DESTINED DESIRES

BILLIONAIRE'S PASSION BOOK 2

ALIZEH VALENTINE

HOT AND STEAMY ROMANCE

CONTENTS

Blurb	v
1. Chapter One	1
2. Chapter Two	6
3. Chapter Three	13
4. Chapter Four	22
5. Chapter Five	29
6. Chapter Six	42
7. Chapter Seven	48
8. Chapter Eight	58
9. Chapter Nine	66
10. Two years later	70
Sign Up to Receive Free Books	73
Preview of The Widow's First Kiss	75
11. Chapter 1	78
12. Chapter 2	84
13. Chapter 3	92
Other Books By This Author	106
Copyright	109

Made in "The United States" by:

Alizeh Valentine

© Copyright 2020 –Alizeh Valentine

ISBN: 978-1-64808-024-1

ALL RIGHTS RESERVED. No part of this publication may be reproduced or transmitted in any form whatsoever, electronic, or mechanical, including photocopying, recording, or by any informational storage or retrieval system without express written, dated and signed permission from the author

❦ Created with Vellum

BLURB

What can I say about Cade Lowell?
I can say that he's arrogant, domineering, and is used to having things his own way.
I would also have to say that he's hot as hell and that absolutely nothing has changed since we broke up in high school—he leaves me just as breathless and frustrated as he did back then, when he was the only one who had ever touched me.
He was just a boy the last time I saw him, but when I return to White Pines to deal with my late grandmother's house, I realize that he's all man now!
I feel electric when I'm around him, and I can tell right away he wants me too, but there's more to love than heat.
Will he ever get past his arrogant ways to see that I want a say in things too?

When Mara's car ends up in a ditch on a snowy night, who should rescue her but Cade Lowell, her high school sweetheart? Sparks start flying, but can they make it work this time?

Cade thought he was over the idea of love and family, but a

chance encounter with Mara, the one who got away, makes him wonder if he can see a future in her green eyes.

Mara's past comes calling in the form of her high school boyfriend, Cade, who's all grown up, rich, and hotter than hell. Can they leave the past behind and find a Christmas romance?

1
CHAPTER ONE

Mara

It was technically still daylight when I left my youngest sister's house in Illinois. She had said goodbye to me, but Chloe hadn't been able to take her eyes away from Alex Reed, who had been standing there all apologetic, desperate to make amends.

They really are cute together, I thought with some amusement. Even if Alex was closer to my age than my sister's, I couldn't help regarding them both with a big sister's eye. *Really, all that trouble over a little romance.*

Despite my amusement, I was happy for my fey little Chloe. Alex would steady her, and she would maybe help him take that stick out of his well-bred, rich-boy ass. He had been nearly silent all through our drive from White Pines to Elgin, so grim-faced and determined to make things up to Chloe that I thought he might pop a vein. All he had wanted was Chloe's address so that he could drive to see her, but I had refused. No way, no how.

Nope, not if she doesn't know you're coming and might be unhappy to see you. I'll drive, or you're not getting a thing from me.

Alex Reed has at least one brother, so he should know what it's like to be simultaneously frustrated with someone and incredibly protective of them. Now here I am, leaving my sister to her happy ending and making the drive north to White Pines again.

Shannon, the middle of us Becker sisters, was probably going to be waiting up for me, and I winced a little at the thought. We still needed to talk about what we were going to do with our grandmother's house, and that wasn't a conversation either of us was looking forward to. Chloe had said she would go along with whatever Shannon and I decided, and I barely avoided rolling my eyes. Of course Chloe weaseled her way out of the difficult decisions and went home with a rich, handsome doctor. Par for the course for Chloe.

I had been hoping to get back to White Pine by eight or nine, but as the sky darkened and large clumpy snowflakes started to fall, I pushed that estimation back, and then pushed it back again. My car, a powerful and elderly Mercedes, drove just fine in the cold and snow, but the snow was coming faster and faster. I saw other cars peeling off the exits, the traffic thinning out, but I kept going.

It'll be fine. I'll just take it slow...

That mantra actually worked at convincing me for almost four hours of white-knuckled driving. I drove slowly but steadily, staring so hard into the swirling white blankness ahead of me that I felt as if my eyes were drying out. Time took on a peculiarly elastic quality. I felt as if I had been on the road forever. It felt as if I would never get to White Pines. Then, miracle of miracles, I saw a sign saying I was just twenty miles away from the city limits.

"Oh thank god," I muttered.

Afterward, I couldn't figure out if it was the release of that vital bit of tension that caused what happened next, or if it was just some strange twist of fate. I was focused on the road, the conditions actually looking as if they were clearing up, and then there was a deer standing stock still in the middle of the road.

As it was happening, it felt as if time stood still. It felt as if I had all the time in the world to look at the deer; to take in its dark eyes, its spindly legs, the round barrel of its body. All of this I saw as I wrenched the wheel to the side with a cry of shock. The deer seemed to wait until the last minute to run out of the way, and when I saw that I had cleared it, I tried to yank the car back onto the road.

With a sense of inevitability, I felt the tires spinning underneath me as the car fishtailed, sliding backwards straight into the ditch. I rocked hard against my seat belt, and for a moment, everything went dark.

THE NEXT THING I KNEW, there was a frantic tapping on the window, and I could see red lights flashing some small distance away.

Oh god, is it the cops?

I hastened to roll down the window an inch. Now I could see the man in the dark wool coat on the other side, a scarf pulled up to protect his face and a knit cap pulled down over his ears.

"Are you all right?" he asked. "I saw your car in the ditch."

My first instinct was to say that of course I was all right, but instead, I took a moment to assess myself. I was definitely bruised and sore, but there was nothing overtly wrong with me. There was no tenderness at all around my head; I had likely simply blacked out from surprise, not impact.

"I think I'm all right," I said, and the man nodded.

"Good. Turn off your car. I'll help you get to mine."

I turned off the engine, and I couldn't help feeling as if I had just pulled the plug on my beloved old car's life support. The thought made me feel oddly queasy, but I shoved it away, looking instead at the man on the other side of the door.

"Are you a cop?" I asked.

"Sorry, no," he said. "But come on, I'll take you up the road to White Pines, at least."

I debated with myself for a minute, and then shrugged. The wind was howling, the car, now that it was off, was cooling off quickly, and I didn't relish waiting for a cop to finally show up.

"All right, just...please don't be a serial killer or anything, all right?"

He laughed at that, and I was surprised by how much I enjoyed the sound of his laughter. When I opened the door, he steadied me in the frozen weeds by the side of the road. I looked at my car, which looked like a wounded animal in the ditch, and sighed. But there was nothing to be done about that now. I followed him back to his car with its hazards blinking on the side of the road, and before I got in, I whipped out my phone and took a picture of his license plate defiantly.

"What's that all about?" my rescuer asked as he got into the car. To my relief, the heat had been left running, and I focused on forcing some life back to my fingertips. Even that short amount of time outside had left them a little numb.

"Texting it to my sister, to make sure that you actually get me to White Pines," I said, flashing him a wide grin. My cocky attitude dared him to have a problem with my precaution. How a man reacted when a woman did something as simple as ensure her own safety was always telling. Some men understood, others got angry. This one laughed.

"Well, you haven't changed a bit, have you, Mara?" he asked. "Still the same suspicious girl with the bright green eyes."

I felt a chill run up my spine as all sorts of explanations for his words tumbled through my mind. My hand was on the door handle when he put the car in drive and pulled away from the edge of the road. If he had moved one moment slower, I might have jumped into the blizzard and taken my chances.

"Who the hell are you?" I demanded, feeling a little defensive—of course I was suspicious. When had the world ever given me a reason not to be?

"You're going to hurt my feelings, darling," he drawled. The car was warming up, and he pulled off the knit cap to reveal a head of thick, dark hair. When he glanced at me, a dozen half-intuited hints fell into place before my brain could fully catch up with what I was seeing. His face was leaner than it had been at eighteen. The strong bones there were starker, but the dark hair was the same, as were the gray eyes, visible in the overhead light.

My hand flew to my mouth, covering it in surprise.

"Cade..." I murmured. My tongue stuttered over his name, but the rest of me remembered well enough. It felt as if a forest fire raced through my body, making me draw a sharp breath.

"Good to see you too, darling," Cade said sardonically, a twinkle in his eyes, and we drove toward White Pines.

CHAPTER TWO

Cade

I HAD NEVER BEEN one to believe in fate, and I wasn't sure that I did right then. I certainly hadn't been thinking of fate when I saw the car in front of me spin off the road; the winking white tail of a deer disappearing on the other side of the road. Instead, my mind had been filled with images of death and blood, and when the woman in the car had finally stirred, I had felt a relief so profound it made me weak in the knees.

After that, all I could think about was getting her to safety and making sure she was well. I had actually liked it when she took the picture of my license plate. There was something about the sharp way she answered me, her take-no-prisoners attitude, that drew me to her like a magnet. That was when I'd recognized her. I'd recognized the sharpness of her voice, the defiant lift of her chin, and of course by those green, green eyes that could take a man apart.

It was Mara.

It was Mara fucking Becker that I had pulled out of the snow, and if that wasn't fate, it was at least proof that the universe had a sense of humor.

"God, Cade," she said, and something in me thought I could hear some kind of warmth in her tone. If there was warmth there, I told myself not to trust it, but Mara had always been a straight shooter...about most things, anyway.

"What are you doing out here?"

"Oh the usual," I said. "Dashing around in the snow, rescuing pretty girls. Being my regular irresponsible self."

God, what the hell was wrong with me? I sounded like a snarky teenager, and she would have had every right to take my head off for it. Instead she laughed a little; a warm sound that made something inside me come undone.

"I'm not going to question it," she said with a light laugh. "I know for a fact that you would have stopped for me ten years ago. The fact that you were still willing to stop now...I think that's to your credit."

Praise from the queen herself. It took effort to stop myself from warming underneath her words. I had been down that path before, and I knew that it didn't lead anywhere good.

"Didn't do it for your approval, princess," I said with a shrug. "I would have stopped for anyone."

"Good," she said, a little tartness entering her tone as well. "Do you want a medal for not checking to see whether a girl is cute or not before you help her out of a wreck?"

I wanted to snap my teeth at her, and that was familiar too. Instead, I ignored her, choosing to focus on driving. The blizzard wasn't too bad, and the reports said that it would stop by two or three in the morning. My car could handle it, but I could end up in a ditch as easily as she had.

In the old days, Mara would have sailed into a fight with her banner held high, or she would have stalked off with way more dignity and verve than any teenage girl should have. Now, though, she simply looked at me through the darkness. I could feel her gaze on me like a touch, and I drew a deep breath into my lungs, letting it out slowly.

When I thought back to Mara and White Pines, I could never escape a shudder of pleasure; always hot, but as I grew older, strange as well. Christ, there had been plenty of women since Mara, the oldest of the Becker girls, but they were mostly gone and forgotten. None of them could draw a shudder from me the way the mere thought of Mara could. Now that she was in my passenger's seat, fully grown and with those same green eyes, those same full lips, I realized I hadn't been imagining it.

I still wanted her, and that thought pissed me off.

"What the hell are you looking at?" I asked, and she laughed again.

"You, of course," she said, and there was no anger in her voice at all. "Are you still so angry at me?"

"I'd have to be pretty insane to still be mad about something that happened ten years ago," I said gruffly. "Christ, we were kids."

"That didn't answer my question," Mara said, but she didn't press. She looked out her window at the sleeting blizzard, and when she spoke again, there was a slightly dreamy quality to her voice.

"I was mad at you for a long time, you know," she said. "I might not have had a reason to be, but I was. I thought...I thought you had ruined a perfectly good thing, but now maybe I see why you did it. Why you left. Maybe it was even good that you did."

That stung more than I thought it would. I could remember my last few nights in White Pines ten years ago. They weren't pleasant at all. The only person that had made them bearable was sitting beside me right now.

"Was I right?" I asked. I had meant for it to come out snidely, but it was a real question. "About what you did, I mean. Did you go to a nice college out east, marry some guy with a portfolio and a perfect credit score at twenty-two, and have an adorable kid by twenty-four?"

"I think you just described the first three or four guys I dated," she said with a little laugh. "But no to the rest. That type of guy tends to want a housekeeper and a nanny more than a partner, and when I figured that out, I dropped out and moved to Atlanta."

I couldn't stop myself from laughing at that, and she shot me a look that was slightly irritated.

"Miss Valedictorian dropped out?"

"As a matter of fact, I did," she retorted. "It was absolutely the right choice. I wasn't meant to work in business administration. I could see that I was surrounded by the kind of people I already wanted to kill at the age of nineteen, and if I'd kept on going with that crowd, I might have actually done it at twenty-five."

"All right," I said, conciliatory in spite of myself. "I'm sure that speech worked on your parents. What did you do instead? What was in Atlanta?"

"A guy," she admitted, so shamefaced that I laughed again. "God, I wasn't even twenty, but I thought he knew everything—it was just dumb. We lasted about ten minutes after I'd moved down there."

"But you didn't move back?"

"No. I had too much pride, but once I'd gotten over that, I'd fallen in love with the city, and by then I'd secured a magazine job. I'm an editor now. It's good work. I can do it on the road when I like. And it pays well enough."

I risked sneaking a look at her again. She wasn't looking at me, and she wasn't expecting me to be looking at her at all. There was a faint line of tension between her eyes.

"But it's not what you want to be doing."

She flashed me a sharp grin.

"What about you? Are you living your dream?" she asked. "Seeing the United States, odd jobs, the great American experience?"

That was familiar. God, I had been ridiculous at eighteen, but a part of me still bridled at her tone.

"You're not the only one who's changed, Mara," I retorted. "I bummed around the country for about two years. Crossed it half a dozen times, worked on a shrimping boat off the Gulf. Then my uncle called me up and told me he had some work for me. I'm in real estate now."

The way I said it, she would have been within her rights to guess that I worked for a landlord somewhere. When she laughed, I bristled, but when I felt her hand move over and touch mine on the wheel, something in me almost purred.

"I thought about you," she whispered, as if it were a confession. "And yes, you were on that damned bike of yours, roaring along the freeway, stopping in towns for a few weeks to get enough gas money to keep going. I can see you on the Gulf, too. I've been there a few times, where the water's so blue it takes your breath away and the sun rises out of it all red, looking like it's on fire...Were you happy then?"

"No," I said bluntly. "It was fun. I had some wild times, but it wasn't right."

"And what you're doing now?"

"Getting closer to right, maybe."

"I'm glad."

She sounded like she meant it, and I had to actually search for the anger I'd always kept right next to my need for her. God, the fact that she could disarm me in less than half an hour would be hilarious if it wasn't so pathetic. I stayed quiet the rest of the way to White Pines, and then I automatically drove her to her grandmother's house.

"Having a family vacation at your grandma's?" I asked as we pulled up.

"No, she's been dead for a few years," Mara said bluntly. Even as calm and steady as her voice was, there was a hurt there that made me want to take her in my arms. "The property got through probate, and now my sisters and I need to figure out what we're doing with it."

She wasn't as calm about all of this as she wanted me to think she was, or that she wanted to be herself, but it wasn't my place to press her. Instead, I got out of the car and went around to open her door for her, and she smiled at me, ever the princess.

"This is where I get off," she said needlessly, but she didn't walk up the stairs toward the door. "Maybe we'll see—"

I could lie and say that I couldn't help myself in that moment, that it was all the memories and need, and maybe just a small urge to rewrite the past. Tell the truth and shame the devil, though, it was only because I wanted her. In the dim porch light, with the snow whirling around us and getting caught in her dark hair, I wanted her—and so I pulled her to me and kissed her.

She tasted as good as I remembered, all warm and sweet, and after a moment of frozen shock, she pressed herself against me. We were both bundled up against the cold, but I could feel the warmth of her rising to meet me. I couldn't stop myself from burying my hands in her hair, holding her still so I could explore her mouth, learning her all over again, showing her how badly I wanted her...

Just as quickly as we had reached for each other, we pulled

away again. We stared at each other, and I realized that I couldn't read her at all. We were adults now, not the crazy kids we had been before. There was an entire decade gaping between us, and despite what some part of me tried to insist, we didn't know each other anymore.

I started to say something, some apology, something to explain away what we had done, but then the door at the top of the stairs opened, spilling a harsh light over us.

"Oh my god, Mara? Are you all right? I've been calling you..."

Shannon, my brain helpfully supplied. Standing in pajamas and a robe at the top of the stairs, she stared at us wide-eyed and confused. There were really no explanations for either of us to make, so I turned to Mara.

"See you later," I murmured.

"Wait," she blurted out, but I was already getting back in the car, heading back toward my hotel on the other side of town. I tried to tell myself that I was in White Pines to do work, not to mess around with my high-school sweetheart; but as I drove through the swirling snow listening to the wind whistle through my windows, I knew that it was only the barest thread of self-control that kept me driving ahead instead of turning around and finding that warmth that I had only ever shared with Mara Becker.

CHAPTER THREE

Mara

"Was that...?"

"Cade Lowell, yes, it was," I said brusquely. "Come on, we need to get inside before the cold gets both of us."

Shannon followed me inside with a frown, and when I stripped out of my winter gear, I could finally breathe a sigh of relief. As I did so, I could smell something utterly amazing in the air, and I turned to Shannon with surprise.

"Did you bake a pie?"

"I did," she said with a slight smile. "And there's some stew as well. I was hoping to eat with you, but there's plenty leftover. You can eat and tell me what the hell happened with Chloe. And with Cade as well, apparently."

I wasn't used to having to answer to people any more, I realized, following her to the kitchen. I worked independently in Atlanta, and I could go days without needing to go into the magazine's office. Even as I noticed it, however, I also noticed how nice it was having my sister sit across from me in our grandmother's old house, ladling out a bowl of stew and cutting off a hunk of thick bread before laying them down in front of me.

"God, Shannon, did you bake bread too?"

"I was on my own all day," she said with a faint smile. "I had to do something, didn't I? Eat, and then talk."

We hadn't been at our best the past little while as we tried to figure out everything with the house. The food and her gentle bullying felt like something of a truce, and I was tired enough that I wanted to take it. The food was good enough that I couldn't even savor it, scarfing it down while putting off her expectant gaze.

Talking about Chloe and Alex was easy. Shannon nodded and agreed that it seemed like they were good for each other, but I didn't miss the wistful look in her eyes. My sister has always been a bit of a romantic, but romance always seemed to pass her by. I could have told her it wasn't really that great anyway, but that conversation never seemed to go all that well.

"So much for Chloe and Alex," she mused. "Now tell me what's going on with you and Cade. Have you guys, I don't know, gotten together again after all this time?"

I winced a little at her curiosity, because if I was honest, I didn't know what to make of it myself. Ever since Cade had picked me up, I felt as if everything in my head had been shaken up; thrown around as if in a hurricane. That shouldn't have surprised me, however. That was just Cade. He came in like a storm, and when he left, nothing was the same.

He had done it to me once before, after all.

Ten Years Ago

"Hey Mara, it's Cade again!"

Sammi, one of my classmates, drew out Cade's name like taffy, shrill and taunting, but underneath it, I could hear her envy clear as day. I shot her a dirty look and walked over to the window, refusing to let myself hurry.

I was acting as cool as I could, but the truth was I couldn't stop my heart from skipping a beat. I had transferred to White Pines to finish out my senior year because my grandma needed some help after a fall. I knew why my parents sent me, but I had figured it would be a dull and lonely time, far away from my family and my friends.

What I hadn't counted on was Cade Lowell, who had stopped me at Malarky's, paid for my burger and then insisted on eating with me. That was almost six weeks ago, and we'd been seeing each other every day since.

He was on that motorcycle of his that made Grandma fret every time he came to pick me up, and he was completely at ease on it. That was maybe my favorite thing about Cade: how easy he was about everything. He was dressed in black jeans, heavy boots, a black T-shirt and, of course, the omnipresent black motorcycle jacket. It was heavy enough to be armor, and that's how I always thought of it.

"What do you want?" I asked with a mock scowl. "Did Carson decide you were too much trouble and fire you or something?"

Cade grinned, unperturbed, open and easy.

"Turns out his kid is getting married tomorrow in Madison so he closed up the garage for the day. I'm heading up to the quarry. Come with me."

"You think I've got nothing better to do than to come with you?" I teased, and his grin turned a little more sly.

"I might make it worth your while," he offered.

I scoffed, but a pleasant warmth was already spreading in my belly, making me want to blush. I pretended to think about it for a minute, and then glanced over my shoulder where a half-dozen other students were fussing over layouts for the school yearbook. I was only there because I had some experience with graphic design, and I was already bored.

"All right, I'll be right down."

I got some glares as I walked out of the room, but it didn't matter. That bright spring afternoon, the only thing I cared about was Cade and getting as close to him as I could.

Cade gave me a helmet and made sure I was clinging tight to him before he roared down the road. Every time I got on his bike with him, I felt a deep thrill of danger and pleasure twine together inside me. When I pressed my cheek to his shoulder, I smelled leather and sweat. I never felt more grown up than I did with Cade.

The ride to the quarry was a short one, and soon enough, we had pulled over onto one of the small side roads that wormed their way all over the area. We left his bike in a sheltered spot and walked hand in hand up one of the narrow paths. He let me walk ahead of him, and I could feel his eyes on my rear and my hips. I knew that if I were at home, my parents would never let me go off alone with Cade. He was my age, and still attended high school for half the day, working the other half, but there was something more adult about him, more dangerous.

Cade and I found a tree with plenty of soft grass underneath, and we curled up on the ground below, my head pillowed on his shoulder.

"How are things at home?" I asked, and he shrugged.

"Dad somehow missed his usual weekend bender, so he's making up for it now. I might just sleep at the garage if he gets too bad."

I winced. Cade's father had a reputation in town, and it wasn't a pleasant one.

"You could come over to my place," I suggested. "There's a spare bedroom."

Cade laughed, shaking himself a little.

"Bet your grandma would love that," he said. "Nah, the garage is good. Its got a TV, some books. No big deal. But I don't want to talk about that right now."

"Oh?" I asked, amused. "What do you want to talk about?"

As it turned out, he didn't want to talk at all, and as way lay curled up under the tree overlooking the quarry, he started to kiss me. We moved against each other, kissing and learning and exploring until all I could hear was our breathing, the slide of our clothed bodies rubbing against each other, our heartbeats thudding as loudly as drums.

I wanted him more than I had wanted anything in my life, but when he started to unzip my jeans, I put my hand over his.

"No," I said. "I don't want that..."

Cade blew hair through his lips, pressing his forehead against my shoulder, and reluctantly nodded. He flopped over onto his back, one arm thrown over his eyes, and I appreciated the opportunity to recover myself.

"Such a good girl," he teased when we had both caught our breath a little bit.

Honestly, I didn't even know why I had stopped him. All I knew was that even if I wanted him something fierce, I didn't want him yet, and I was grateful that he seemed to understood.

After a while, we curled up next to each other again, kissing a little, talking more. I listened with half an ear as he talked about getting on his bike to see the country, going from town to town, learning all the ways people were alike and all the ways they were different. I was more worried about my grandma and how frail she seemed with every passing day.

When the sun started to inch toward the horizon, he took me back to town, dropping me off in front of my grandma's house.

"I'm going to be working on a project for the next few days, but maybe I could see you on Friday?"

"Sounds good," I said. "Sure you won't agree to scandalize the neighborhood and stay in our spare bedroom?"

He laughed.

"Nah. I'm good. See ya, princess."

Friday night came, and I ignored the school chatter about the upcoming spring dance. It all felt very far away to me: all of the talk of who was going, who wasn't. Instead I went home, checked with my grandma to make sure she had taken all of her medications, and went to read on the porch for a while.

Around dusk, just as I was getting ready to give up and go inside, I heard the thunder of Cade's motorcycle. I put my book down and rose up to meet him, a wide smile on my face. When he dismounted and wrapped his arms around me, I felt as light as a feather, like a bit of ash thrown up from a bonfire drifting back down to earth.

"Hi," I said softly. "What do you want to do tonight?"

He grinned at me.

"Want to go to Chicago?"

I blinked, laughing in half-disbelief.

"What, you mean like...for the weekend? Cade, you know I can't leave my grandma..."

"No, not for the weekend, maybe for like a week. There's a guy down there that needs all the hands he can get for some kind of production push, and then after that, I don't know. Maybe down to New Orleans. I've always wanted to see the Gulf. I think my mom's people were from there. Or Los Angeles. Why not?"

I stared at him, because despite the sheer insanity that was spilling out of his mouth, there was a part of me that wanted nothing more than to get on his bike with him. I had to push back from him because I was suddenly so tempted I couldn't stand it.

"What the hell are you talking about, Cade?" I hissed. "Are you leaving? What about...what about school? What about graduation?"

Cade's face hardened.

"If I want a diploma, I'll get a GED, but I don't want one. I don't want to stay one more minute in this damn town. I've been spending the last few days getting things together, getting some cash, packing up, and now all I need is for you to come with me."

The confusion that been bubbling up inside me swiftly turned to anger, and I glared at him.

"You mean that you decided to do this just a few days ago, and now you expect me to drop everything and come with you?"

The look he gave me was impatient. He reached for my hand, but I pulled away.

"Come on, Mara, you know you're too good for this town. You know that you want to come with me."

"I *know* that I'm graduating from this damn high school in a few months, and I *know* that I need to stay here and look after my grandmother," I snapped. "I thought you knew that, but apparently not."

He looked a little guilty at the mention of my grandmother, but he refused to back down.

"I want you with me," he said. "We would be awesome together on the road, you know that. I don't want to do this without you."

"But you will," I said sadly, reading the decision in his eyes. "Because you've decided, haven't you? I either come with you now with absolutely no preparation, no regard for my responsibilities, and no safety net if everything goes wrong, or it's over."

Cade looked stricken, but I refused to quit.

"God, Cade. You can't do this to me. You can't just make a decision and insist that I fall in line like some kind of doll!"

"That's not what I want," he growled. "You know that. I want us to get out of this damn town, and I want us to be ourselves. I want to be with you, and I don't want to be Daniel Lowell's son who's probably going to end up just like him if I don't get the hell out."

"You can't ask me to do this," I repeated, and to my dismay, he took a step back. When I reached for his hand, he shook me off.

"Fine," Cade said. "You want a life that you can predict down to the millimeter? You want to go to a nice college and marry a nice man and live out in the suburbs wondering where the hell your life went, fine."

He turned away, striding back toward his bike, and this time, I was the one who tried to hang on to his hand.

"Cade...don't..."

He glanced back at me, and his gray eyes were so angry that I fell back a pace. I suddenly remembered all of those people who had said that Cade Lowell had a temper, who had told me he could be violent and cruel, and for the first time I was afraid of him.

"You told me what you want, princess," he spat. "And that's fine. If that's the way you want to live your life, fantastic. That's not what I want for myself."

I was so stunned by his words that I was completely mute as he got on his motorcycle again. I watched as he gunned the bike down the street, and even though I knew most of the neighborhood was watching me, I stood on the drive and stared after him long after I was gone.

"You never told us about any of that," Shannon said quietly, eyes wide.

"Well, I stayed at Grandma's for most of that summer, and then I moved home for all of two weeks before I started college." I shrugged. "It didn't seem like there was much to say. I think maybe Grandma told Mom about it, but it wasn't something that Mom and I ever discussed."

"I wish you hadn't been alone with that," Shannon said, and I sighed.

"I've never been all that good at spilling my guts," I said. "I just wanted to...I don't know. Not forget it, but put it away maybe?"

"And now Cade's back, and you're back..."

"He seems so angry still," I mused. "I know he was pretty angry after he left, but shouldn't he have gotten over that? It was so long ago."

"Who knows?" Shannon shrugged. "Just because he's back doesn't mean that you have to do anything about it. If he doesn't care for you, you don't have to care for him. You can leave each other be."

She rose to take my empty bowl of stew, setting my reward of pie in front of me. We talked about other things: the endless discussion about what to do about the house, how Chloe was doing, and throughout all of it, I couldn't stop my mind from sneaking back to Cade.

I don't know if Shannon knew that leaving Cade alone was easier said than done. From the moment we met, we had never been able to leave each other alone if the other was near; not until he rode away from me that spring night almost a decade ago.

Now that we were both in White Pines again, who knew what would happen.

CHAPTER FOUR

Cade

I DID PRETTY WELL MAINTAINING my self-control. I waited a full three days before I drove down to the house where I had dropped Mara off. It was one of those bright days that you get in December; not a cloud in the achingly blue sky, and the morning frost burned off before noon.

White Pines had always been a sleepy little town, but there was interest in it now. More and more folks were flying north for the winter, enchanted with the idea of having a classic holiday worthy of a Hallmark movie, and I was interested in taking advantage of it.

The truth was that I had fought going back to my hometown. I knew it was going to be an amazing professional opportunity if I got in on the ground floor, especially for someone knew the town as well as I did. There were a lot of ways to get rich here, and I certainly didn't mind adding to my considerable fortune.

My uncle always said you could never be too rich, and after he taught me everything he knew, I had to agree.

I was surprised that White Pines hadn't had much of an effect on me. I was prepared to be deluged by bad memories from long ago the minute I drove past city limits at the beginning of December. My dad had died a handful of years ago, and after I cleared out his apartment, I had never given it a second thought. Now I was back, driving past my old high school, Malarky's, all the old haunts, and I didn't feel anything

Well, most of the women who'd ever spent more than a few days with me had called me a cold bastard, and I was fairly comfortable with them being right about that. Then I turned down the street to Mara's house, and I realized that all my musing had been completely wrong.

It felt like all of those emotions I thought I'd left behind as an idiot teenager were just waiting for me there at that house. There was the anger and frustration, of course, but beyond that there was an anticipation I hadn't felt since I was eighteen and head over heels in love with Mara Becker. It was joy and excitement and the complete certainty that I had found the girl who'd been made for me.

In short, it felt like being an eighteen-year-old again; one who knew absolutely nothing about love and nothing about women. That's what I tried to tell myself anyway.

However, when I pulled up into the driveway, I felt the overwhelming familiarity of being in love with the aloof and ferociously intelligent girl from another state. I choked it back, because technically, I was there on business, and instead of dwelling on my nostalgic feelings I walked up the drive to ring the doorbell.

Mara answered almost immediately, and for a moment we simply looked at each other. Seeing her out of her bulky winter coat, it was even easier to remember her as she was ten years ago. She was still tall and generously curvy, her breasts and her hips filling out her casual green dress and her dark leggings with ease. A dark green cardigan covered her shoulders, and incongruously, pink bunny slippers covered her feet.

"I think that pink doesn't quite go with the rest of it," I pointed out, and she grinned at me briefly.

"Shows what you know. This look is all the rage in Atlanta," she retorted with an affected pompous tone. "What are you doing here, Cade?"

"I come in peace. Can we get out of the cold?"

Mara hesitated for a moment, and that hurt more than I thought it would. Then she nodded, and stepped back to let me in the house.

"I just finished having lunch, but would you like some coffee?"

"I'd love some coffee," I said, following her in to the brightly lit kitchen. As we walked, I couldn't help but notice that her grandmother's house had good bones. It was a classic, solid wood, with hardwood everywhere. It was slightly shabby in the best way, as if people had lived there and loved it for years.

With a faint start, I realized that that was exactly what had happened. It was something that plenty of people would pay to experience, and for a moment I felt oddly ashamed of myself.

"You don't need to worry, you know," Mara said, breaking my reverie. "Grandma's been dead for a few years now. She's not going to pop out of the woodwork to grill you on your intentions."

She stopped a moment, considering her words.

"Though Shannon might. She's away for the moment, though, so you should be safe."

"I'm glad to hear it," I said with a laugh. "And no, I wasn't worried about your grandma. I was just noticing what a beautiful home this is."

Mara nodded as she set up the coffee before turning to look at me. Her green eyes were as sharp as diamonds, and I felt as if she were taking me apart molecule by molecule. It probably says something about me that it turned me on.

"So I spent some time on Google," she said, and I blinked.

"Good for you?"

"I mean, I looked you up. And I found you in some very impressive databases, I have to say."

"What, were you expecting to find a criminal record?"

She shrugged, a faint smile on her face.

"You've done quite well for yourself. Your real estate company is worth billions."

I grinned.

"My uncle got me started. I just went bigger and better."

"I saw. It's impressive, even if it doesn't really jibe with what I remember."

I thought I might have heard a note of censure in her tone.

"People change," I said, and she nodded.

"They do. You did. I certainly did. So do you believe that enough to remove whatever stick you have up your ass about me?"

She looked at me expectantly, and I couldn't stop myself from laughing out loud.

"You really are something, princess," I said. "All right, clean slate?"

A troubled look crossed her face briefly, and I wanted nothing more than to kiss it off of her. Then it passed, and she smiled at me.

"Something like that. And I want to know why you're here. I didn't think you were really the type to linger."

"Ouch. Well, all right, cards on the table. Do you realize that you're sitting on a very lucrative investment property?"

Mara raised her eyebrows.

"You mean the house? Is this about me telling you that we were having some trouble deciding what to do with it?"

"Yeah. White Pines was a sleepy little place when we were teenagers, Mara, but it's not going to stay sleepy. The holiday getaway industry is booming, and when people think about the perfect holiday, White Pines is exactly what they're looking for. White Pines could be on the verge of an enormous boom in seasonal tourism, and people are looking for houses just like this one."

There are plenty of people that would be thrilled to hear news like that, but Mara only gave me a considering look.

"And what are you proposing that Shannon, Chloe, and I do with this gold mine?"

"Not so much what you would do, but what I would do. I can't make any promises, not without an inspection and some forms filled out, but I've been looking for houses in the area that look just like this one."

"And once you have them, what are you going to do?"

"Spruce 'em up a little and then either sell them as vacation homes or lease them out as the same. A little Christmas cheer for the family for the price of a grand or so a day."

She blinked at that amount of cash, and I grinned.

"Oh believe me, there are plenty of people who will pay for the kind of perfect holiday they never got to experience as kids."

"And what about you?"

"What about me? I told you, I'm putting in cash to—"

"No, not that," she said, setting two steaming cups of coffee in front of us and taking a seat. She slipped her bare feet out of her ridiculous slippers and locked them into the bar under her chair.

"I meant, would you pay a grand a day for that kind of perfect holiday?"

I hadn't expected to be ambushed by the long forgotten

dreams of my eighteen-year-old self while I was in White Pines, and I sure as hell hadn't expected to be ambushed by the dreams of an even younger self; one whose dad drank away all the money for Christmas presents and who saw people going home with fresh Christmas trees and wondered if he could go with them.

"Well, you know what they say. If you're selling, you probably shouldn't be buying," I hedged, and it felt suddenly as if those green eyes were looking right through me.

"I see. So you're selling an illusion, something that makes you roll your eyes and laugh."

"Can't do much without a sense of humor," I said.

"I think I see our problem," Mara said. "You want people to buy an illusion. What my sisters and I are selling here, well, it's something real."

"Something real?"

"Oh yes," Mara said with a small smile. "Something very real. We came up here every Christmas with our parents, and we spent a lot of summers here as well. We grew up here. I spent my last semester in high school here taking care of my grandma. She got better and enjoyed another five years, and it wasn't because of me, but I know I helped. I fell in love with a boy for the first time here, and I got my heart broken here too. So when you come along talking about selling an illusion...well, it doesn't sit quite right, does it?"

"You have a price," I said flatly. "It might be higher than I'm willing to pay, but you have one."

"Of course I do," Mara said. "Everyone does. But I just want you to know what you are asking for, and why your pitch doesn't do much for me right now."

I had dealt with tough sells before, but Mara wasn't trying to raise the price by playing on my sympathy. She was just telling me what the house actually meant to her, and that plucked a string somewhere in the vicinity of my heart, one that I had thought was permanently stilled. I sipped the coffee—surprisingly good and beautifully hot—and thought for a minute.

"All right, I'm going to do three things. First, I'm going to write a number on this piece of paper. This is the minimum of what we would pay for this house. This is a number that I'm giving you sight unseen. When I see more of it, it could go up.

"The second thing I'm going to do is ask you to come with me and see what we're doing at some of the other properties I've acquired in town. You told me about this house's past, now let me show you what its future might look like."

Mara was nodding thoughtfully. That was always one of the things that had made her stand out, even ten years ago. She was someone who wanted to think about what was coming, what it meant.

"That seems fair. I will tell you, though, that if you're trying to pull a fast one on me I'll say no out of spite, and my sisters can't budge me when I get like that..."

"I'm not trying to pull something, and if I did, you could be as spiteful as you wanted to be. Does that sound good?"

"So far, so good. You said three things. What's the third?"

"Third, I'm sorry to pry, Mara, but when you mentioned the first boy you fell in love with, and the first boy who broke your heart...was that me?"

I wriggled my eyebrows, thinking that I was being funny and that she would laugh and maybe smack my arm, shaking her head. Instead, Mara took on that peculiar stillness that she had, that way of looking more like a statue than a person. It was as if she had gone somewhere far away, with no plans of returning until she knew it was safe.

"Of course it was you, Cade," she said softly. "Of course it was."

CHAPTER FIVE

Mara

CHRIST, why the hell was I doing this?

I knew why, of course. The number on the piece of paper that Cade had passed to me was actually double what I'd thought it might be, and the idea of that price increasing made me dizzy. Even Shannon, the one who was most reluctant to sell the house, had nodded and said that I should at least go with Cade and hear him out.

"I don't think it will do any harm to learn more about what he's offering," Shannon had said. "But if you have the least doubts, Mara, don't worry about saying no. We'll figure something else out."

The problem was, of course, that I was less worried about what Cade was selling than I was about Cade himself. In the last three nights leading up to the day we'd agreed to meet again, I had found myself troubled with dreams. I'm not much of a dreamer, usually. I just close my eyes and wake up again after seven or eight hours. The last few nights, though, I had woken up with a head full of Cade. We had never gotten much beyond some fairly fevered groping and some very good kissing, but my dreams were far more explicit. I dreamed about him naked, I dreamed about how he might look at me naked, I dreamed about touching and kissing a lot more than we ever had before.

This morning, though, I had woken up from one of the strangest dreams. I had been moving through a fog, and I was calling Cade's name. The only sound that came back to me in that strange and unpleasant place, however, was an echo of my own voice. By the end of the dream, I had simply sat down on the ground to cry.

I was restless all day, and when seven o'clock rolled around, I felt like I was wound tighter than a spring. It might have been easier if Shannon was willing to come with me, but she begged off, deciding to stay home and do some touch-up painting in the living room.

At seven sharp, Cade texted to let me know that he was here, and when I walked out, he opened the car door for me, smiling a little.

"The garage still has your car?" he asked.

"Yeah. They'll be done by tomorrow at least."

"Good." He paused, and when he spoke, there was a touch of reluctance to his tone. "I'm glad to see you, Mara, though I'm sorry your car had to take a header into a ditch to make it happen."

"You know, it's funny, I thought about contacting you on Facebook a couple times. Do you know it recommends you to me sometimes?"

Cade blinked.

"Really?"

"Yeah. It's freaky. Sometimes I'll be talking with a friend about who knows what, and then there's your face."

"Why did you never try saying hello?"

"I don't know," I confessed. "I guess I thought we were too different, or that too much time had passed. Something."

"And now?"

"And now I know even less. I still feel this...anger surrounding you." There had always been something about Cade that made me feel like I could just tell him whatever was on my mind. It looked like that, at least, hadn't changed.

"I'm not angry at you," he said too quickly, and I shrugged.

"Let's see what you want to show me. Your great vision."

It was safer to talk about houses and visions. It was too easy to stray from the safe topics and to venture into territory that was too dark by far, and the more conversations I had with him, the easier it became.

We talked a bit about human migration patterns and the need for comfort wherever one lived, but then suddenly Cade said something that startled me.

"Do you remember the Driscoll's old place?"

"I do," I said. "That was abandoned when we were kids, right? And then some kind of cult moved in?"

"They weren't really a cult, just a bunch of hippies who wanted to have a good time. The lady who owned the house finally got sober, and after she started a nice quiet life in Anaheim, she wanted to sell out. I picked up this property a while back, and it's a perfect representation of what I'm thinking might be in store for White Pines."

The neighborhood around the Driscoll place was older than the area around my grandma's house. There was a lot of lawn around the houses, and they were a bit larger, a bit grander. To my surprise, when we pulled up into the driveway, the house was lit up from the inside and the porch lights were on as well.

"Cade, does someone live here right now? Are we interrupting some poor family at dinner?"

"Relax. No, no one lives out here. I worked with a designer after we got the house back to code. It was fun, in a weird way. We wanted to be able to show people what they could have in White Pines, what their families could have. Come on."

Almost instinctively, he took my hand as we walked up the sidewalk to the front door. It made sense, I thought. The night was getting chillier, and our breath made plumes of steam in the cold air. He unlocked the door, and for a strange moment, I had a vision of him carrying me over the threshold like a new bride.

He took my coat, and as he led me into the living room, I looked around in surprise.

"Oh, Cade," I murmured.

It was like something out of a storybook. When he had described a display house, I had thought of something sleek and obviously designed by professionals. I imagined textiles from across the world and exotic woods. That would have made sense, and that would have been very attractive to a certain kind of wealthy investor or buyer.

Instead, this felt like a place a family lived. The furniture was harmonious but mismatched, and there was just a touch of wear on everything, making it look very well loved. The rug on the ground was felted wool of the same kind that my grandmother had, and there was a single pane of stained glass looking into the dining room, perfect and lovely.

"Beautiful, isn't it?" asked Cade. "The girl I got to do this is a wonder. She does a lot of antique sales, estate sales, and she can create just about anything..."

"It's definitely beautiful," I said hesitantly, and Cade cocked his head at me.

"But?"

"Let me see the rest," I said. "Let me see this Cade Lowell holiday vision."

He shrugged and led me on a tour of the house. Every room was like the living room: beautifully furnished and looking like a happy family had simply stepped out for a minute, perhaps to see the lights along Main Street. As we walked through the house though, I could feel something squeezing at my heart. I'm pretty tough about most things, but something about the house with its beautiful homey touches made me want to cry.

"So?" he asked in the living room again. "What do you think?"

"So this is what you want to sell to people? Fake happiness?"

He blinked at me, narrowing his eyes.

"This isn't fake, Mara," he said. "The families that will come here to stay are real. This is a setting for them, a place for them to have a good holiday trip. A happy, memorable holiday."

I wanted to ask Cade then if he had dreamed of houses like this when he was kid; if he had hoped and prayed that he would have a place that was as calm and as beautiful. It would have been the cruelest thing in the world to ask, because I knew that the answer would be yes.

"This feels strange to me," I said, my voice a little gentler. "I can't imagine someone moving right in and deciding that this is okay for a week or two weeks or a few months and then just leaving."

"Well, of course you wouldn't be okay with it," he said. "This place was never designed for someone like you."

"Someone like me?" I asked. "What do you mean by that?"

Cade grinned a little, sideways and crooked, and I felt my heart beat a little faster. God, that he could do this to me after all this time was downright unfair.

"You thought you were going to go to college, settle down somewhere and have a family—do all the right things. Instead you ran all the way to Atlanta to work in magazines. Even your version of rebellion was practical. I know there has to be something else you yearn for, some other reason you felt the need to upend your life and do away with your careful plans. What is it, Mara? Do you want to be in a band? Do you paint? Something about you has always struck me as artistic..."

"A novel," I said, a little nettled. "I haven't told my sisters about it."

But I had told him. There was something oddly right about it.

"Right, a novel. Whether we had this growing up or not, it's not something we need. I don't know if the people who like it need it or not either. I know that they want it. They'll be pretending too."

"And what will they be pretending?" I asked. There was something oddly magical about this place; the soft way that Cade was talking, the warmth of the house after the harsh cold outside. Whatever kind of magic it was, no matter how artificial or how strange, I took a step closer, wanting to embrace it.

Cade looked around, and if there was any part of him that was sad not to have had this kind of life for real, he didn't show it.

"Oh, any number of things," he said. "I mean, if I used this as my getaway, I would be thinking that I'd never left White Pines at all, and that there was some alternate reality where that had turned out all right. Maybe I got a decent job somewhere close by, up at eight, home by six, steady work, good money. And of course, it would all be worth it because I'd get to come home to this."

I nodded, because I could see where he was going with this. Hell, I had felt the tug of it myself from time to time.

"And I would've moved up here after college instead of going to Atlanta. Might have gotten a library science degree and when Mrs. Penske retired—"

"She'll never retire. She'll die behind the desk and then her ghost will run that place," Cade interjected, and I shushed him.

"Fantasy, remember? When Mrs. Penske retired, I took over for her. I love running the summer reading program, and every day I help people find the books they know they're going to love."

Cade took a step closer to me.

"Is that what would make you happy?" he asked huskily. "Finding people the books they would love to read?"

I laughed a little self-consciously. What was it about this man that made me want to bare everything?

"Sort of. At least, I think I would enjoy it. As to what would make me really happy? Maybe publishing my novel."

I expected Cade to express polite interest, or, if he was feeling a little mean, to laugh. Instead, his face lit up as if Christmas had come early.

"Really? You have a novel already? Is it something you're letting people read yet?"

"I...almost. I almost have a novel. I'm maybe forty or fifty pages from the end. Something like that? I... You can read it if you want."

"That would be our first fight," Cade said with a laugh. "I want you to take more time off from the library to work on your novel," he said in a serious voice, playacting as if this fantasy were real.

"And I think that it's way better to go into the Christmas season with money to spend. We have a lot of family, both of us."

We really didn't. Cade had been on his own since long before it was appropriate, and I really only had my sisters. The thought sent a pang through me, but it also made me remember that little Chloe was pregnant and probably getting married soon, if the looks between her and Alex were anything to go by.

Cade shook his head, slightly rueful as he looked around. He had been the one to create all of this, but the reality was as distant for him as it was for me.

"So it seems we even fight in fantasy land," he mused.

There was something melancholy about it, so sad that I came up behind him. He startled a little when I wrapped my arms around his waist, leaning my cheek between his shoulders. He was taller than I was, a full six feet to my own five-eight, but he was so much broader and stronger. I fit against him perfectly.

"That's life, here or in fantasy land. If we never fought, were never angry with one another, or if we never had anything to work out, how would we ever know when things between us were really, really good?"

"You think times would be really, really good, Mara?"

"Sure. Here in fantasy land, anyway."

He turned, and I wondered if I had made a mistake. It had seemed companionable, even sweet, when I came up to hug him from behind. When he turned around, however, there was something much more intimate about it. He was so close to me, and I could feel his warmth reaching out to me even through our clothes. It was as if we were burning for each other, and I wondered about fate and inevitability.

"In fantasy land, fights end with a kiss," he said, his voice unsteady.

I knew that the smart thing to do would have been to back off, to laugh and end the silly game we were playing. We had been too old to play house even back when we met as teens, and we were far too old for it now. As adults, we understood consequences and chemistry, and we should have been more wary of heartbreak and hopeless entanglements.

"Well, I hate to break the laws of fantasy land," I murmured, and I tilted my face up for his kiss.

It was no chaste peck on the cheek that he gave me. Instead, his powerful arms went around me, drawing me crushingly close, and his lips captured mine with a nearly ravenous hunger. With that kiss, in a single moment, my inhibitions fell away from me, and I knew the only thing that mattered in that moment was what I felt in Cade's arms, what he could make me feel.

He kissed me as if the world was coming to an end, and before I even knew I had done it, I had wrapped my arms around him, drawing him as close as I could. He reached up to cradle my cheek with his hand and turned my head slightly, seeking the sensitive skin close to my ear. When he latched his teeth into my earlobe, I gasped, but I couldn't stop myself from pressing close against him, feeling helpless and squirming against him in desperation.

"This is entirely too much clothing," he gasped, pulling away, and it was the smartest thing I'd ever heard. What followed was an ungraceful shedding of our winter clothes. They were dropped on the floor like fallen autumn leaves, and our frantic pace only slowed once we were both naked. Then we stopped entirely, our eyes greedily taking each other in for a minute.

Cade had filled out since I had last seen him, and I had never seen him naked then. His body was corded with muscle, and a thin trail of dark hair ran past his navel, stopping just short of his cock. My eyes widened when I saw his erection, already hard for me and jutting away from his body.

I wondered how he would see me. I wasn't seventeen anymore. There were stretch marks and scars, all the marks a decade could bring. If I had any fears about what he might have thought, however, they were banished by the look of utter worship in his eyes.

"God, princess, you're gorgeous," he breathed, and then we were back in each other's arms. This time, I could feel his erection pressed against me like a burning brand, so hot that I couldn't resist taking it in my hand, circling him with my fingers before drawing on the velvety skin.

Cade groaned, burying his face in my hair. He thrust into my hand with an abrupt motion that felt just short of desperate. I thought he might take me right then, throwing me to the ground, but he pulled away.

"Hey!" I cried out. It was his right to stop this madness if he wished to do so, but at that point, I couldn't even pretend not to be heartbroken over it.

"If you keep that up, I'm just going to bend you over the dining room table and take you," he said roughly.

"I really fail to see the problem with that—" I began, but then yelped as he scooped me up in his arms, bridal style. I had always thought I would be too ungainly for anyone to carry like that, but my arms naturally went around his neck, and I knew he wouldn't drop me, not in a million years.

"I have a better idea than that," Cade said, and he carried me to the master bedroom.

Like the rest of the house, the master bedroom was decorated with an eye toward care and comfort. When Cade flicked on the small lamp on the dresser, the room was bathed in an amber light that revealed an enormous bed, made up with crisp green-striped sheets and a cozy blanket folded neatly at the foot. It looked like the perfect place to sleep away a cold winter night, but the last thing I was thinking about right then was sleep.

When Cade set me down on the bed, he didn't join me right away. Instead he stood back to look at me, and I looked back at him. There was something solemn about that moment. It felt as if we had created more than just a fantasy land; as if we were actually in some other world, some place where he had never left me behind, where I had never refused to come with him.

"I think I have compared every woman I've ever been with to you," he said finally, and I shook my head.

"Unkind," I murmured, "but maybe I know what you mean."

When Cade finally joined me on the bed, he moved more

slowly. His kisses, though still passionate enough to singe, took on a considering quality. He was learning my body intimately, using his mouth, his hands, his tongue—and he would not be rushed. When I tried to reach for him, he pushed me back onto the bed.

"Later," he muttered thickly. "Right now, I just want to savor you..."

I couldn't keep my hands off of him entirely. Instead, I threaded my fingers through his dark hair, tugging gently when he hit just the right spot. I whimpered when he reached my nipples, tugging gently on the peaks with just the right combination of pressure and sweetness.

His clever tongue licked a path from my sternum to my navel, and then he was nuzzling between my legs, lapping at my folds until my body opened for him as naturally as a flower would for the sun. About that point, all metaphors deserted me as he spread me open and started to lick for real.

I had never really cared for this act all that much, but on the bare edges of my consciousness, I wondered if it was because I had never met a man who enjoyed it as much as Cade appeared to. There was nothing tentative about the way he devoured me, nothing shy or cautious. Instead, he lapped fiercely at my clit while plunging a finger partway into me, withdrawing and then repeating that motion. When my hips bucked up against that sudden shock of pleasure, his free arm clamped over them, holding me still so he could do whatever he wanted with me. Apparently what he wanted was to make me shout.

My fingers tightened in his hair. I must have come close to yanking some out, but somehow I stopped myself. My heels dug into the mattress underneath me, craving more, but Cade was on his own time. He wanted to make me feel good, and he was utterly single-minded in the pursuit of his goal.

The pleasure washed over, leaving me shaking, but it all felt so good that a sudden spike of it caught me by surprise. It rose up and up in the core of me, drawing me tight, and I managed to find my words.

"Cade...Cade, if you don't stop, I'm going to..."

Cade laughed, and somehow I could feel the vibrations through my body, which only added to the sweet fire that coursed through me.

"Why the hell would I ever want to stop?" he asked, and then he lowered his head again.

There was a part of me that wanted to hold out. I wanted this pleasure to last, but Cade wasn't having it. He drove me higher and higher until I hit that peak, and then I was falling. I heard myself cry out, and it seemed as if every muscle in my body was tightening. Even if I had wanted to, I couldn't get away from the pleasure he was giving me. Instead, all I could do was allow it to take me.

I was only starting to come back to my body when Cade came to lie down next to me. I tried to shape some kind of question in my head, but then he pulled me on top of him. There was a roughness to his actions that told me he had been holding off for quite some time, and now he simply couldn't hold back. His strong hands clamped over my hips, and he lifted me as easily as a feather. I braced my hands on his chest, marveling at his strength, and together we guided me down on top of him. Just feeling the tip of his cock at my entrance made me whimper a little, and when he was fully sheathed inside me, I cried out with pleasure again.

"Oh my god," I murmured, and he stilled, looking up at me.

"Are you all right?" he asked, his voice harsh with need. I knew he would stop if I needed him to, but right then that was the farthest thing from my mind.

"Yes. Oh yes, Cade, I just need you...so much..."

He groaned at my words, and his hands tightened reflexively

on my hips. He drew me back up for a moment, and then he plunged into me full length again, making us both cry out in pleasure.

He moved like a man driven insane with need, lifting me as if I was made just for him, just for his pleasure. I couldn't stop myself from moving with him, urging him onward with every sound that I made.

There was no one in the world who had ever felt as good as Cade did right then, and after the thunderous climax he had brought me, I longed to give him the same pleasure.

I felt the low tremors start in his body, perhaps even before he did. I raised and lowered myself over him more quickly, with more force. A thin sheen of sweat covered me, allowing us to slide against each other with ease.

Cade's eyes opened suddenly, dark and wild.

"Not going to let you go again," he growled, and then with a roar, he pressed inside me one last time, shaking hard. I closed my eyes, feeling every bit of him, and I knew that I had never stopped loving Cade. Not really.

CHAPTER SIX

Cade

IF I'M BEING COMPLETELY honest, I had imagined this more than once. As it turned out, actually making love with Mara left any shower daydreams or late night jerk-off sessions in the dirt. The girl of my dreams had turned into a woman made of fire, and the minute we were done, there was already a part of me that was eager to know when we could go again.

She whimpered softly, sliding off of me to nestle naturally at my side. I reached over to brush her hair back from her face, and as I did so, I could feel a ripple of anger roll through me at what might have been.

Christ, it was ten years ago, I told myself, but that didn't stop me from rolling away from her and getting to my feet, preparing to leave the bedroom to grab my clothes.

"So... is it part of your fantasy to be a salary man who has to get back to work late at night, or are you just naturally bad at cuddling?" asked Mara. Her voice was confident and amused, and I wondered if she was laughing at me. To be honest, I wondered how long that question had been lingering in my head.

"We shouldn't have done this," I said shortly. "This was just supposed to be business."

I glanced back to see her eyes narrow. In the dim light of the room, the green turned to black, and there was something sharp and merciless in her gaze.

"Really? For someone who wants to keep this all business, you sure did have a good time a few minutes ago..."

"Of course I had a good time." I bit off the rest. *Because it was you.* "Get out of bed and let's get dressed, Mara. You've seen what I've got going on here, and you can decide for yourself whether you want in."

Mara looked as if she would do as I said for a moment, and then she sat up.

"No."

I paused halfway to the door and turned back around.

"Wait, what?"

"No," she repeated accommodatingly, rolling up to her feet. She was gloriously comfortable in her nudity. She set her hands on her generous hips and looked me in the eye.

"I'm not going anywhere until you tell me why you're still so angry. I mean, sure, sometimes I think I should have gone with you too, but I was still in high school. If you can't see why a high school girl shouldn't blow off graduation, her family, and all her plans just to join a guy who thought that it might be fun to head south for a few months, I don't know what to tell you."

I glared at her. I'm pretty damned intimidating when I glare, but Mara just ignored it. Instead, she looked at me, imperious as a queen, and waited to see what I had to say for myself.

The anger that had been hiding inside my heart for the

better part of a decade bubbled to the surface, and I couldn't hold it in any longer. Why not tell her? Why not try to see what she had to say for herself.

"I saw you," I said roughly. "The day after."

She scowled at me.

"Saw me? What are you talking about?"

"The day after you said no," I bit out. "I was going to leave that night, but I couldn't. It wasn't school, it wasn't my dad, it was you. It was just...you."

I could feel something rough in the back of my throat, but somehow I managed to keep talking. There was nothing in her face to give her away, just a confused frown and sympathy. No guilt. And that surprised me.

"I rode around all night and that next day, thinking. Maybe I should stay. Maybe we could work something out. Next evening, I went back to your house."

She blinked.

"The next..." she was lost in thought, trying to remember a different time. "That was the spring dance."

"Yeah, the spring dance," I said. "How long did it take you to find a date after I left, Mara? Did you cry over it for an hour or so, and then go back and take your pick of the guys who were drooling over you? Or were you seeing him behind my back the whole time we were together?"

I expected...I don't know what I expected. Maybe she would stutter and deny it, or maybe she would come back and tell me I had no say in anything she did after we broke up that day. Instead, for a moment, her eyes lit up with fury, and she reached for one of the pillows we had pushed off of the bed.

I barely knew what she was doing with it before she chucked it at me as hard as she could, right at my head.

"Goddamn it, do you ever stop and question something before you write it in stone?" she growled.

I caught the blanket she threw at me next and frowned at her.

"What the hell—"

"Of course I wasn't seeing anyone else when we were together! And leaving aside the fact that you left me—that *you* left *me*—you have no right to question what I did afterward. Leaving all that aside, you blind idiot, my grandmother got me that date."

I blinked.

"What?"

She crossed her arms over her breasts, glaring at me and fuming like a volcano.

"I went to the dance with Andrew Langston, whose girlfriend had just dumped him. His mom and my grandma were friends, and when his girlfriend dumped him right before the dance, Mrs. Langston asked my grandma if I would do him a favor."

"And you said yes?"

She glared at me.

"I might have had some experience with getting dumped abruptly," she retorted. "I might have had some reason to be sympathetic toward him."

I could feel the world tilt slightly—like the past I had built my life upon was shifting, and everything was sliding back and forth. With Mara's explanation, that anger drifted away, leaving me feeling raw and strangely renewed.

"You...didn't just find a replacement?"

"No!" she exclaimed, throwing her hands in the air. "You must have seen us during the first hour of the dance. I had to borrow a dress from this older girl that Mrs. Langston knew. She was built like a stick, and I thought that at any moment I was just going to, I don't know, burst out of it. We went to the dance, we danced one dance together because it seemed like the thing to do, and then for another hour we moped on the sidelines.

Then we went to Malarky's and talked about our respective relationships failing."

"You didn't do anything else?"

She gave me a sharp glare.

"Oh, you mean the part where we checked into a seedy motel and fucked away our sorrows?"

I couldn't control the brief flash of hurt, rage, and utter credulity I felt when she said that, and she rolled her eyes.

"Dear god, Cade! Do you really think you're that easy to get over?"

Then an expression of shock took over her face. She stared at me as if she had never seen me before. I felt even more bare than I already was, standing there naked—I felt stripped to my very core—and my first instinct was to take a step back. I didn't want her to see me this hurt over something that had happened ten goddamn years ago. I didn't want her to see the things I thought on my darkest nights.

Then she was crossing the space between us as if it was nothing. Ten years, thousands of miles, two very, very different lives. None of it mattered at all. All that mattered were her arms around me, her warm face pressed against my bare chest.

"Mara..." I meant to push her back. I should have. I didn't want her to pity me, but instead all I could do was hold her close.

"I swear to you, Cade, when you left, I thought the sun had gone out of the sky. I was furious, both at you and at myself."

I blinked, distracted for a moment.

"Why were you mad at yourself?"

"Because...oh, for a lot of reasons. Because maybe I should have gone with you. Maybe I should have figured things out and found a way for you to stay. Maybe I should have been a better girlfriend, and then you never would have left at all."

"Hey, that wasn't...You were a great girlfriend. I mean, there was a reason I wanted you to come with me..."

She grinned up at me, and somehow, she wasn't afraid to show me how hurt she had been ten years ago. That day had left a mark on both of us, and I could sense that she remembered as much as I did.

"Well, I know that now," she said with her usual practicality. "Didn't really get it when I was just a kid. Two months out, I was moping all over the place and driving my family crazy because I refused to say why."

"Two months after I left White Pines, I was in Detroit," I admitted. "I came really close to getting into some very nasty trouble."

"I'm glad you got out. I'm glad for everything that happened that got you back here this month."

The way she said it startled me, and then I realized that she was entirely right. With everything that was going on in both our lives, with all of the trouble we had both been through and all of the history we had with this town, it was nothing short of a miracle that we had made it back at the same time. Even less likely that we had found each other on that lonely stretch of road.

This was a second chance that no one deserved, but that against all odds, we had been given. As she led me back to bed, a slight smile on her red lips, I realized I had to hang on. I barely believed in second chances; I knew I definitely wasn't going to get a third.

CHAPTER SEVEN

Mara

I STARED at the page on my laptop accusingly, as if staring at it long enough was going to unlock the secrets that would make me a real writer. My laptop was predictably mute, and no magic words came out to get me to the next bit of action. Instead my characters were in limbo, and I felt that if I stared at the screen any longer, I would go stark raving mad.

It was a few hours past sundown, and there was a velvety quiet over everything. I thought it would be the perfect time to work on my novel for a while, but I hadn't been making all that much progress.

"Hey, Mara?"

I looked up to see Shannon in the doorway of the little office I had always claimed as my bedroom when we were staying at Grandma's. She looked somehow irritated and amused all at once, which was something.

"What's up?"

"Cade Lowell is throwing pebbles at my window," she said. "Unless you really, really pissed him off and he thinks he has a chance with me, he's probably trying to get your attention."

I blinked.

"Okay, I'll go out and deal with it," I said, blushing just a little at Shannon's laugh as I passed her by.

"Well if you two want to do something that'll put you on Santa's naughty list, I'm going to a choral concert tonight. There's a free one at the community center."

"You're getting pretty settled in here," I commented, and she shrugged.

"Maybe after we sell the house, I can get an apartment here or something."

"You could keep the house," I suggested, and she shook her head.

"No, too big, too many rooms. What the heck am I supposed to do with all this? If someone was going to keep it, it should be Chloe. She's the one with a baby coming."

I let it go. It was a conversation we had had a few times, and we were still no closer to solving it. None of us really liked the idea of our grandmother's house passing to strangers, but none of us were quite sure what should be done with it either. As I headed to the front door, I was happy to put the matter behind me for at least a little while. Cade was waiting in the yard, and he greeted me with a wide smile.

"Hey, you know that was Shannon's window, right?"

Cade frowned.

"Really? I could have sworn that was yours..."

"It wasn't even my window when I was seventeen," I said with a grin. "Did you want something? Or should I get Shannon out here and let her deal with you?"

Cade walked up the porch steps and wrapped me in his

arms. It felt so good that I stayed in his embrace for a short moment, but then I headed back into house, tugging him after me with a grip on his scarf.

"Brrr, it's too cold to be out there without a coat."

"So get a coat," Cade said. "I'm taking you out tonight."

I blinked at him. This was the first I had heard of it.

"Really? Where are we going?"

"Well, did you know there's a French restaurant in White Pines now? White tablecloths, red wine, the works. I snagged a reservation for tonight, but there's plenty of time for you to get into something nice."

I stared at him. Being taken out to a nice French restaurant seemed like it should be any girl's dream, and I felt a little ungrateful for not being immediately enthused, but I hadn't planned for it at all.

"I was working on my novel, actually," I hedged, and Cade shrugged.

"You've got plenty of time to do that later, don't you? Come on, you're going to love this place."

I frowned at him, pulling away and making no attempt to go up to my room and change out of my sweatshirt and yoga pants.

"A please would be nice," I pointed out, and Cade looked startled.

"What's the matter?" he asked. "I figured you would love some French food after spending a few weeks in White Pines."

There was something derogatory about the way he mentioned the town, and it raised my hackles a little. I may not have spent as much time in town as he had, but I had spent enough, and I decided I didn't really like how he was talking about it.

"As a matter of fact, I'm having a pretty good time eating at all the places I remember, and French food is fine, but I prefer to eat it when I'm in good company."

Cade scowled, crossing his arms over his chest. It made him look even more imposing, but I wasn't feeling in a mood to be imposed upon.

"What the hell is that supposed to mean?" he growled, and I glared right back at him.

"What that means is that I prefer to be asked when it comes to deciding what I'm doing, not told, and that as a matter of fact, I do have something better to do than to be dragged to dinner with a man who thinks that he's always in charge."

"I do not think I'm always in charge!" Cade snapped. "I was trying to do something nice for you!"

"Cade, you know I don't like surprises—especially when they interfere with plans I've already made. Next time maybe ask if you want to do something nice for me," I said, and he threw up his hands, walking out the door as quickly as he had come in.

I stood still, feeling as if I had just weathered a hurricane. Making a low, frustrated sound in my throat, I threw my hands up in the air and stalked back to my room.

Shannon appeared in my doorway a moment later, dressed all in black with sparkling earrings dangling from her ears. Right, choral concert, I remembered.

"Was that you and Cade I just heard?" she asked, wide-eyed. "Is everything okay?"

"Everything is just peachy," I growled. "As it turns out, you can't teach an old dog new tricks, particularly when that old dog's favorite trick is to always get his own way."

Shannon raised an eyebrow.

"Should I ask?"

"No, probably not. It's just stupid. I'm sure we'll work it out."

She nodded, and ten minutes later, I heard her car start and head down the driveway, leaving me alone. Of course by then, I had resigned myself to staring at my novel some more, changing a few words here and there and hating all of it.

I couldn't stay focused on my writing because my brain kept returning to Cade and the spat we'd just had. I'd told Shannon that we would work it out, but what in the hell were we working out? What were we doing? Were we friends with benefits? Were we boyfriend and girlfriend? Something more, something less?

More importantly, would he ever learn that the last thing I ever wanted was to be led? I knew plenty of women who loved the idea of being taken care of, of having a guy take the lead, but most of them also had no problem making their own decisions at the end of the day.

In the last ten years, I had spent plenty of time dating and plenty of time being single, and what I had learned was that I liked getting my own way, too. Sure, if I was in a relationship, I could cede some of the control, compromise, figure out how to find something that would suit all parties, but I had never wanted to give it up entirely.

In a dark mood, I wondered what would happen if I told Cade that I wanted to be the one to make all the decisions from here on out. I would be the one to decide where we would eat, what we would do. I knew that he would like it as little as I did, but maybe it would get the point across.

I jumped a little when I heard a shower of pebbles against my window. When I opened the curtains, I saw Cade standing in the lawn, a large paper bag in one hand. With a frown, I opened the window.

"What are you doing back?" I asked. "Don't you have a reservation at a French restaurant to get to?"

Cade grinned, white teeth flashing in the light from the house.

"Pull your claws back in, Mara, I come in peace. I thought that maybe if you didn't want to go out, I could bring some food back to you. Truce?"

I thought for a moment, and when my stomach rumbled, I decided that a truce sounded like a great idea.

"Truce. Come meet me by the back door, it's closest to the kitchen."

When I opened the kitchen door for Cade, he startled me by dropping his head down to plant a gentle kiss on my forehead.

"Sorry," he said. "You're not an employee, and I shouldn't boss you around like one—nor do I want to."

"Really? If you are taking your employees out for French dinners, maybe I have a few more questions for you."

He laughed, setting the food on the counter, but his face was serious.

"I have a bit of a problem where I like to be in charge, I guess," Cade admitted. "Works just fine when I'm actually paying all of the folks around me. Works less well with you."

"Yeah, unless you start paying my salary, you're going to have to ask permission, or at least for my opinion," I said absently. "What did you bring?"

"Believe me when I tell you that the folks at the French restaurant weren't all that keen on packing me up a takeout order," Cade said. "I got them to pack up a little bit of everything though. I think that's the duck."

It was in fact the duck, dark and fatty and delicious, and I admitted to myself that yes, it was a little nicer than yet another burger at Malarky's. We took the food, some plates and some silverware into the living room, and with the TV turned on to something light and brainless, we devoured the food. It wasn't the most glamorous date, but there was something companionable about it: sharing food, pointing out what the other should try, talking about the places we had been.

"Oh my god, that was so good," I said with a sigh, leaning back on the couch. "Next time you should let me pay, and by next time, I mean tomorrow at the latest because that lamb was amazing."

"First, you're not paying for anything, and second, I'll bring you food whenever you like. I didn't realize you were working on your novel, and I'm sorry I tried to take you away from it."

I shot him an amused glance.

"Let me pay sometimes," I said. "You're not actually my employer, remember?"

He looked like he might argue, but then he shrugged.

"You know I don't try to dominate things because I think you can't handle them, right? I don't buy dinner because I think that you can't."

I tilted my head to look at him. There was something thoughtful on his face, and that was new. The Cade of ten years ago had been a lot of things, but contemplative definitely hadn't been one of them.

"Then why do you do things like that? I figured it wasn't for some kind of bullshit macho reason, but I'd be curious to hear what it really is."

"I want to make sure you know that I can do all those things for you now," he said. "That I've got plenty of cash, or that I'm tough enough to handle things, or smart enough. Something like that, anyway."

My mind flashed back to Cade and myself ten years ago, standing just a few dozen yards away from where we were sitting right now. He had looked so arrogant on his bike, demanding that I drop my entire life and come out to the open road with him. Maybe now I could see that it wasn't arrogance at all.

"Cade, I read up on you. No one is going to question how much cash you have or how tough you are now."

"I know that," he said with a slightly lopsided smile. "There was a time when I was younger when I wanted to prove it to the world. Now..."

"Yes?"

"Now I just have to prove it to you."

The words were calm, stark, and threaded with absolute truth, and I couldn't resist the urge to curl up closer to him, bringing him in for a sweet kiss. There were a thousand things I wanted to say to him just then. I wanted to tell him that he had nothing to be ashamed of, and that he had nothing to prove to me at all.

"You don't," I said softly. "You really, really don't."

"Because you know me so well after ten years away from where we were?"

I thought about it a moment and then shook my head.

"Who you are shines through," I said softly. "It... gleams. You're something special, Cade, but I've always known it. I know who you are. Sometimes, it feels like I've always known."

Cade pulled me close to him, a little rough, and I realized that his hands were shaking a little.

"Cade?"

"It's always been you," he said, his voice slightly hoarse. "Is that strange? No matter where I went, who I met, what I did or how much money I made; in the back of my mind, you were the one that I wanted to understand me. You were the one I was trying to impress."

The honesty in his voice, rough as old leather, took my breath away. When he reached up to caress my cheek, I leaned into it. I felt something soft and quaking inside me, as if we had gone too far together to ever be apart. My heart whispered that it was love. My brain tried to pull us both back.

"You don't need to impress me, Cade," I said, laying a soft kiss on his palm. "You just need to...to touch me. To be with me."

His reply was to draw me closer for a kiss, and despite the fine tremors that ran through his frame, I could feel how gentle he was, how he handled me as if I was something infinitely precious and frail. In other circumstances, with other men, that might have been something that frustrated me. I could take a little bit of rough handling, and sometimes I craved it, but right then, in the silence of this house, I wanted to be precious to him.

"Are you done?" he asked softly, and I nodded.

In response, he tugged me up from the couch and let me lead him back to the room where I was staying. It was only a twin bed instead of the luxurious king we had shared at the Driscoll's house, but we bundled ourselves into it neatly. We didn't need space between us just then.

It felt as if we spent an eternity kissing. There was something about it that reminded me of high school, when we were both full of nothing but wild longing for each other, full of breathless need for things that we couldn't even name yet. We weren't high school kids anymore; we were adults, and we had seen more of the world, been burned, and maybe done a bit of burning ourselves.

It felt as if we were making up for a decade of missed kisses. Cade's hands wandered my body, exploring and claiming. I was so eager for him that it felt like forever before he worked his way under my clothes, and when he found my warm skin, I squeaked a little with the cold.

"Sorry," he said with a brief chuckle.

"Here, give me your hand..."

When he offered one hand to me, I kissed his knuckles and then his palm, brushing my lips across the sensitive skin there and between his fingers. He made a brief noise of surprise, and I purred a little. I felt him shift a little against me, and I felt his cock get harder through his jeans, as if his entire body was paying attention to me now.

"Mara..."

I slipped his first two fingers into my mouth, making him hiss with surprise. I watched him through lowered lashes as I sucked on his fingers, lapping at the sensitive tips with my tongue before pulling them in deeper. He couldn't take his eyes off of me as I worked over his fingers, eyes that nearly glowed with hunger.

"God, do you have any idea what you do to me?" he asked, and then he pulled his fingers away.

"Likely the same thing you do to me," I said with a smile. As Cade leaned in to kiss me again, I knew that he had always been a part of me, always been with me. He had been locked in there all this time, and now that he was here, with me, I never wanted to let him go.

Silently, we stripped and came back to each other in the bed. The passion was rising between us again, and sooner rather than later, it would consume us.

As we kissed, growing more desperate with every passing moment, I closed my eyes, sending a silent prayer up to anyone who was listening.

Please. Please, I want him. I want him, and I love him...

CHAPTER EIGHT

Cade

I HAD ALWAYS THOUGHT that this time of the year went fast in the business world, but the speed at which Christmas came hurdling toward me and Mara was completely overwhelming. It seemed like days flew by in the span of a few hours, and I wondered if this was what happiness was like.

I guess I'd always assumed that I was happy. I was happy on my own, and I was happy working for my uncle and then building my fortune. Good looks and cash: once you've got that, you've got it made, as far as most people are concerned.

I didn't realize how devastatingly lonely I had been until I looked over at Mara the night of the disastrous French dinner. We were crammed into that tiny bed after wearing each other out, cuddled as close as we could get. Her cheek was pressed against my chest, and she had one arm thrown over my waist as if she owned me. She murmured a little in her sleep, a frown marring her forehead, but she quieted and calmed when I reached up to stroke her hair. She made a contented noise and snuggled closer to me.

In that moment, I realized a few things. The first was that I had never been entirely happy before that moment. Not in all my life. She felt like Christmas morning every day, like some precious treasure I had to keep safe.

The second thing I realized was that I loved her.

It was like lightning striking. The world felt different after I realized it, and after that, there was no way that I was sleeping. I loved her, and nothing would ever be the same. This was the real thing. This wasn't something I was selling to people who were too busy to do much beyond work, and this was the thing that people might search for their entire lives and never get.

At some point I dozed off, but I awoke again close to dawn. There was a chill to the air, and in the night we had both burrowed under the covers. With a silent sigh, I disentangled myself from Mara and the blanket, tucking her back in as soundly as I could before reaching for my clothes.

"Mmm, why don't you come back to bed?" Mara asked blearily. "It's too early for much of anything."

I chuckled a little, evading the grasping hand that snaked out of the covers to drag me back.

"Unfortunately, I really can't stay in bed with you all day, much as I would like to," I said. "Work needs to be done, and if I stay with you, I'll just be deliciously distracted."

"So be distracted. I figured one of the benefits of having all that money was getting to work when you wanted to and being free to do as you pleased the rest of the time."

"You'd think that, wouldn't you? Later though. Later we'll have all the time in the world."

I nearly caved and told her what I was thinking of right then and there, but somehow I stopped myself. She didn't do much more than tug at my shirt sleeve petulantly when I leaned in for a kiss, and before I had closed the door behind me, I could hear her breathing level out.

I sneaked through the house toward the front door, but I needn't have bothered. Shannon Becker sat curled in the living room with a cup of coffee in her hands, and she raised her eyebrows at me when I paused in the hallway.

"There's some coffee if you want some," she offered. "Sorry, I don't know what the etiquette is for running into your sister's date first thing in the morning."

"Well, assuming you don't run me off with a shotgun, I'll say that we're all doing well," I said. "And yeah, coffee is good too."

The coffee was surprisingly good, and Shannon wandered into the kitchen to watch me as I poured myself a mug.

"I tend to think that Mara can handle her men," she said, "but then there's you."

I turned to her with a curious expression on my face. Shannon and Mara didn't look much alike. Where Mara was all hourglass curves, dark, dark hair and tumultuous green eyes, Shannon was plainer, quieter.

"If you think Mara can't handle me, I'm pretty sure you're wrong."

Shannon's smile was thin.

"I think she thinks it," she said. "You did a number on her ten years ago."

There was something razor sharp about Shannon's words, and I frowned at her, sipping the coffee and trying to keep it from burning my throat.

"Are you...threatening me?" I asked, because in her plaid bathrobe with her hair in a messy bun, Shannon didn't look very threatening.

"I would if I thought I could bring anything scarier than

Mara could," Shannon admitted. "Really, shotgun speeches are more her area than mine."

"Ah. So what's your area?"

"Just telling the truth, I suppose. Mara acts really tough, but the truth is that you hurt her. She never told anyone about you and what happened, did you know that? She kept it from all of us, and she used to tell us everything. I think you hurt her too much for that."

I stared at Shannon, wondering if she was laying it on thick, but she looked utterly serious.

"I didn't know that," I said, and she looked carefully into my face. Mara was all motion, but Shannon had a gift for stillness. Finally, she nodded.

"All right. I think you'll do the right thing and treat my sister right. At least, I hope you will."

SHANNON'S WORDS stuck with me the rest of that day. The thought that I'd be able hurt Mara, not just anger her, not just irritate her or frustrate her, was still slightly incredible to me. Because that meant she cared about me—cared about me a whole lot. It made me feel like even more of an ass for making that long ago mistake about her spring dance.

Mara and I talked on the phone and texted constantly in the days leading up to Christmas Eve, but I wasn't able to see her again. I told her I was busy, and that was the understatement of the decade. I had never really thought about how much effort it took to put an empire on hold, but it required all of my attention.

The key to making the money I had in my career was constant diversification, and putting the right people into key positions of power. When I called, they answered, and in a series of meetings involving various concerned and surprised people, I let them know that I would be taking a step back from everything. They would be in charge of the day-to-day affairs, and unless an actual emergency arose, this was going to continue indefinitely.

When one man, who I had put in charge of all Florida operations, asked me privately if everything was okay, his worry actually looked foreign to me. In my mind, I was already living in another place, another world with Mara. It would be perfect, and there was a chance I might never go back to what I had been doing before. If that was the case, some of these arrangements might become permanent.

I shook my head and told him there was nothing to worry about. I had simply changed, and it was time to do something else.

After the meetings were finally over, I finally had time to do what I had held in the back of my mind the entire time. Some of the arrangements were very quick, but others took a little longer. It took all of the resources I had at my disposal to get everything ready for Christmas Eve, but I did it.

I showed up at Mara's place just after dark.

This time, she knew I was coming and that I was taking her out. She met me at the door in a shimmering lilac gray dress that made her eyes even greener, and the smile she gave me made my heart beat faster.

"Are we all good?" I asked teasingly. "You can tear yourself away from your novel for a little while?"

"All good," she said with a grin. "God, but it's good to see you. I've been missing you for days."

She hugged me tight, and the kisses we exchanged were on the verge of going from sweet to passionate in a moment. As much as I wanted to take her back upstairs, I had plans for the evening, so I pulled away.

"I've missed you more than I can say," I said warmly. "I'll try to say it though if you like. Go on and get your coat. I made reservations for us at the French restaurant."

We talked of small things on the drive over, and it occurred to me that she had no idea what was coming. There was no artifice to her at all, nothing that expected a single thing from me besides me being myself.

This was right. This was perfect.

We ate the delicious French food, and when I asked her if she was ready for dessert, she grinned at me.

"You know I always am," she said with a smile. I gestured at the waiter, who nodded and brought out what looked like a globe of dark chocolate decorated with swirls of white. She looked at it quizzically, not quite sure what to do with it, and I nodded at her.

"You break it," I supplied. "There's a surprise inside."

"So it's like an enormous Kinder Egg," she said with a grin.

She cracked the top off the chocolate globe with a spoon, and with a surprised look, she drew out two tickets.

"Cade, what's this?"

"First class tickets to Beijing," I said with a grin. "I have a house there, and we can leave whenever you like. Hell, we could be in Beijing by the day after tomorrow if you wanted."

She stared at me.

"And what are we going to do in Beijing?"

"Whatever you like," I said expansively. "Work on your novel, see the sights, drive out into the country to see what that's like. Mara, these last few weeks have been amazing. I want to be with you, and I want—"

"You want," Mara said heatedly, and to my shock, she stood up, laying her napkin to one side. "I'm seeing a distinct theme here, Cade."

She stalked out of the restaurant, leaving me so shocked that for a moment I just let her go. Then I hurried after her, throwing a few hundred down on the table to pay for the meal. I caught up with her in the frigidly cold parking lot, and before she could go another step farther, I grabbed her arm.

"What the hell, Mara? You can't just storm out on me like that without some kind of explanation."

She whirled on me, jerking her arm out of my grasp. Her eyes were brilliant in the lights of the parking lot, a green so hot they almost burned.

"Explanation? All right, I'll give you an explanation, Cade, but I don't know how much good it'll do because you don't seem to hear it, ever."

"What are you—"

"This is just like when we were seventeen," Mara cried. "You think you can go ahead and make all kinds of decisions and that I'll be happy to go along with them. You think that I'll drop everything in my life just to follow you around on whatever adventure you've got cooking."

"This wouldn't be just my adventure," I protested. "This would be ours—"

"No, it's yours," she spat. "You decided on Beijing, you bought tickets..."

"Christ, I can buy tickets somewhere else..."

"Don't bother, I'm not going! If this is how you want to live your life that's fine, but you'll have to find someone else to do that with—because it's not for me."

Something dark in me reared its ugly head, and I glowered at her. I wasn't sure how this had all gone so wrong, but it had, and that stung worse than I thought it would.

"Does it feel good to be the one saying no to everything, Mara? Is this the closest thing to power you ever get to feel?"

She gaped at me, but I tore ahead, heedless of the shocked look on her face.

"Do you get off on turning away from things? Is it because

I'm not good enough for you? Is it because you're afraid of taking risks? You've always got responsibilities and plans to follow, but I can't help but notice you're the only one making them."

"What are you—"

"You're always so rigid. You're always doing what other people think the right thing should be. Sometimes, that right thing seems to keep you from doing anything daring, taking any risks at all. Sometimes that right thing isn't right for you at all!"

Mara clamped her jaw shut with a snap, and to my shock I could see there were tears in her eyes.

"Leave me alone," she said. "If you don't let me walk off right now, I will call the police and have you arrested."

Her threat shocked me less than her tears had, but I still froze where I stood. I watched as she stalked to the end of the block, and after a few strokes on her phone, a cab came and picked her up, leaving me alone.

CHAPTER NINE

Mara

CHRISTMAS DAY dawned bright and crystal clear. There was a thin blanket of white snow on the ground, giving White Pines a sparkling glamour that should have brightened anyone's day, but I was far from a space where I could be cheered up. I had stumbled into the house the night before, walking straight past a stunned Shannon to shut myself up in my room.

I'd cried so hard that my head still felt a little sore. Eventually, sometime in the middle of the night, Shannon, armed with soup and some actual fresh-baked cookies, got the whole story out of me. She looked sad, but not surprised, and somehow that made it worse.

"I thought he had finally figured it out," I said, drinking some water to try to re-hydrate at least a little. "I thought...I don't know."

"You thought he saw you and not just what he wanted to

see," Shannon said, squeezing my hand gently, and I smiled at her a little.

"God, you're smart," I said. "You should have been the writer."

"I'll leave that to you," she said, wrinkling her nose in a surprisingly adorable way. "I'm just happy enough to bake cookies and be moral support."

Shannon had always been so sensitive to what Chloe and I were feeling. She left me alone the rest of the evening, and the next morning, she made sure that I had a breakfast of toast, bacon and eggs waiting for me as soon as I got up.

"This is good, thank you," I said blearily.

"I have some presents for you too, but you can open them tonight," she said with a smile, and I smiled back a little.

I was going to say that she was getting some gift certificates, but then there was a knock on the door. I stiffened and Shannon went to look.

"It's him," she called back to me. "Should I just tell him off?"

That made me laugh. That was usually my job, and I shook my head.

"You're a good sister," I said. "I can handle it."

"All right," she said, heading upstairs. "But if you need anything, just yell."

There might be some yelling regardless of whether I needed anything, I thought. Wishing that I was wearing something more dignified than ratty pajamas and a robe, I opened the door.

Cade was dressed in the same blue suit he had worn the night before, and there was something hollow in his eyes. He stepped in the house without waiting for an invitation and looked at me for a long moment.

"What do you want?" I asked, unable to resist adding, "Would have thought you'd be in Beijing by now..."

"I was wrong," he said bluntly. "Completely wrong. I

shouldn't have tried to kidnap you away again, and I shouldn't have just assumed you were coming with me."

"Why did you think I would?" I asked, feeling my heart tie itself into a knot. I cared about him more than I had ever cared about anyone, but this wasn't a fight I could have over and over and over again.

"Because I would have gone for you," he said, the words pouring out of him. "Because I love you, and I thought...I wasn't thinking at all. I want you, and I love you, and I need you with me, Mara."

I stared at him, frozen with shock, my hands flying to my mouth.

"I love you too," I choked out. But when was love ever enough? "But Cade, I understand that you like adventure, and I don't want to stop you from living your dreams. I don't want you to not go to Beijing if that's what you want. But there's so much I need to do, so much, and if you can't—"

"Pick a place."

"What?"

"Pick a place, anywhere in the world. I don't care if it's Bangkok or Paris or Ulaanbaatar. I don't care if you want to stay for a week, a month, a year, or even an hour. I don't care about going to Beijing—I don't care about going to any one place. It was never about going to Beijing, it was about going somewhere together, so we could have an adventure *together*. So we could start a *life* together. I understand why you think this is just like ten years ago, but I promise you I get it now. So name any place. I will take us there, and I will stay with you. Just...please, Mara. Believe me."

I stared at him, and it all clicked into place. I could see now that my past hurt may have spurred my anger the night before—it had just felt so familiar. But things were different now—Cade was different now. I knew this wouldn't be our last fight, and that we might each still have a bit of pain from our past to work through, but I couldn't resist him any longer. I threw myself into his arms, and all I could say was that I loved him over and over again. We could get through anything, together.

"Where to, princess?" he said, and his voice sounded as coarse as sandpaper. "Anywhere in the world, you name it. It's up to you, forever…"

"We can figure out a place together. That's all I care about, that it's you and me, together. Anywhere in the world, as long as I'll be with you," I whispered, and I knew that that was the most important thing.

10

TWO YEARS LATER

Cade

"Are you going to stop looking at your reviews? We're landing in just about twenty minutes."

Mara glanced up from her phone long enough to lean over and give me a kiss.

"Two more good ones, and one that's a bit meh, but the meh review belongs to some guy who actually thinks the earth is flat. But all right, just for you, I'll put it away."

"My wife, the famous novelist," I said with a grin. "Are you giving everyone a copy of your novel for Christmas this year?"

"It'd be easy enough, but no," she said, snuggling next to me. "It's just gift certificates again. Call me boring, but nothing says love like convenience and cash."

The private jet that was taking us from New York to Wisconsin was comfortable, but the truth was that I couldn't wait to be on the ground. After Paris, Milan, and Moscow, it felt strange to be excited by a little town like White Pines, but there it was.

"It's been an amazing time," I said softly, stroking Mara's hair.

"What, listening to me bitch about reviews the whole way from New York?"

I thought about the last two years, the give and take that had grown between the two of us as we realized that instead of either of us being in charge, we could simply rely on each other. She had taught me more about love than anyone else in the world, and this was the reward—Mara curled up next to me, gazing at me with wry adoration and her signature brassiness.

"All of it," I said with a grin, and I pulled her in for a long kiss that only ended when the flight attendant told us it was time to fasten our seat belts.

The End

SIGN UP TO RECEIVE FREE BOOKS

Sign Up to Receive Free E-Books and Audiobook Codes.

Would you like to read **The Unexpected Nanny, Dirty Little Virgin** and **other romance books** for **free**?

You can sign up to receive these free e-books and audiobooks by typing this link into your browser:

https://www.steamyromance.info/free-books-and-audiobooks-hot-and-steamy/

Or this one:

https://www.steamyromance.info/the-unexpected-nanny-free/

PREVIEW OF THE WIDOW'S FIRST KISS
A BILLIONAIRE AND A VIRGIN ROMANCE (DREAMS FULFILLED BOOK ONE)

By Scarlett King

Blurb

The afternoon that the mistletoe sprigs appear all over town, impoverished military widow Lorena Webster is about to spend her last twenty dollars so that her daughter Cindy can at least have one Christmas gift. As they walk down to the toy store from the apartment they share with Lorena's sister Andie, they happen to see Lorena's longtime man crush window shopping up ahead.

James Norris is a heartthrob actor turned billionaire producer who returns upstate every year to visit his family. He's shopping for a replacement gift for his mother, after accidentally leaving her Tiffany lamp at home, when he notices the lovely young mother in the inadequate coat coming his way. Caught under the mistletoe, he's startled and amused when the little girl in her arms leans over and kisses his cheek as she passes by.

Lorena and James quickly connect as the determined Cindy plays Cupid. But there's just one problem: James's meddling ex Andrea Case is using his family Christmas as a bid to get him back—and she has James's gullible mom on her side.

Lorena

All I want for Christmas is to give my little girl any Christmas at all. Since my husband Manny died in Afghanistan in a military operation that couldn't go on his record, I never received any death benefits, or even a body to bury. For two and a half years, we've been living on the edge of starvation while I work two jobs and scramble to save our house. It's been hell—and I've done everything in my power to shield my little girl from the worst of it.

But then comes the day when my baby girl leans over to kiss a random stranger under the mistletoe while I'm walking by. The stranger turns out to be *the* James Norris, a hot Hollywood producer worth more money than anyone could ever spend. And the weirdest part of all is—he's wonderful. And he likes me. When he promises me and my little girl to give us a proper Christmas after all, I wonder if I'm getting a second chance at love—and life.

James

When the prettiest young widow in the world comes walking into my life with her adorable daughter, I fall pretty damn fast.

I've put my career first for most of my life, and now that I'm past forty, I'm starting to wonder if it's time to think about all the things I sacrificed. Like having a family. Having a sweet face to wake up to in the morning, and loving arms to fall into at night. Lorena just might be the right person to fix all of that for me.

Winning her over is going to take some work; she has a baby daughter to protect, along with her own broken heart. But that's not the complication I'm worried about. My ex, expert gold digger Andrea Case, is inserting herself into my family's Christmas celebration, manipulating my mother into making sure she can stay. Is she going to ruin Christmas? Or can I find out a way to save it for all of us?

CHAPTER 1

Lorena

Twenty dollars has never made me feel so happy. It's December 23rd and finally, after months of scrambling to keep the heat on and have food in the fridge, I have twenty dollars leftover to buy my baby daughter, Cindy, a Christmas present. It hurts to be this grateful for something so small—especially when Christmas dinner will be a cheap takeout pizza—but it's still a relief, something I haven't felt in months.

So when I walk out of the front door with my two-year-old nestled in my arms, a thick wool blanket wrapped around us both to make up for our inadequate jackets, I'm distracted enough by our good fortune that I don't notice the mistletoe at first.

Phoenicia is one of those tiny little towns in Upstate New York that survives on being pretty, having touristy shops and venues, and having the only late-night gas station for several miles. It has a bed and breakfast, a theater, a fifties-style diner, boutiques, an old German butcher, and a whole lot of drafty old Victorians. One of those drafty Victorians was left to me in my aunt's will, so Cindy and I moved here from Long Island after my husband, Manny, died.

Getting the house was a bittersweet, survival-level stroke of luck—but a big one, with Manny's benefits tangled up in red tape for over two years. I wouldn't be so scared if it was just me, but I have our daughter to worry about too—to keep warm, sheltered, and fed. I swore on Manny's grave that I'd do my best job. Cindy is the one steady light in my life, and as usual my focus is on her more than anything else as we walk along the sidewalk—up until everything starts going weird around us.

I smell the fresh scent of cut mistletoe first—that slightly astringent smell, mixed with the slightly piney perfume of the berries. I'm used to catching whiffs of it all through the Christmas season, but as I draw near the main street, the wind picks up and blows the overpowering smell of the plant into my face.

I stop, eyes watering from the wind, and look around in confusion. The smell is so intense that it's almost like someone's burning a pile of the stuff. I look around and see no fire, but abruptly notice the sheer quantity of the stuff. Mistletoe is hanging everywhere, all over town.

Every doorway, the corners of every house and awning, the arching light displays running over the streets, the lampposts, everywhere that a sprig of mistletoe can hang, at least one dangles, hung by a red ribbon. I start moving slowly toward the closest one, not entirely sure what I'm seeing.

"Mommy, what's the smelly green stuff?" Cindy is immediately fascinated, but I gently steer her out of grabbing distance of the sprigs. The stuff is poisonous, but the berries smell nice. Bad combination around a tiny kid.

"It's mistletoe, honey. People kiss under it. See?" I point to an elderly couple smooching while a couple of Millennial girls take their picture, looking charmed. The couple is pretty cute. I wonder how many decades of marriage they have under their belt—and then I remember Manny and look away, my heart stinging.

"Oooh. Is it magic?" Cindy sounds excited. Magic is her thing. Her favorite stories are fairy tales—even the creepy ones.

"I don't know," I reply honestly. I'm that way about everything: magic, prayer, Santa, karma, God. I've always believed that any kind of religious opinion or paranormal belief should be sorted out by individuals, and not fed to them by their parents.

I also never want Cindy thinking that I know everything, or that I never make mistakes. No pedestal for me means less chance of disappointing her later—a consideration I wish my parents had given me. Not that I would ever leave my daughter to drag me to bed at night because Mommy and Daddy had too much happy juice, but still.

It's the middle of the day two days before Christmas, and of course the streets are jammed with last-minute shoppers. There's a toy store two blocks down that has plushy snowshoe hares. That's what Cindy wants: a snow bunny. Fifteen dollars plus tax, and enough change left over for a bag of Christmas candy.

Unfortunately, I'll have to push through this gawking crowd to get to our destination. It's not going to be easy—because like me, they're shocked by the sudden appearance of all this ... greenery. And that means they're mostly standing around, blocking my way.

They're either standing around talking about the mistletoe, or bustling around trying to clear it from their properties, sweeping small piles of mistletoe into the gutters—and yes, some of them are standing around kissing under it. It's very cute and kind of ridiculous, and I wonder how many people had to get together early this morning to pull this prank. Not to mention, who they were.

There's a man leaning against a lamppost on the corner as I cross the street. It takes me a moment to recognize him as Jack Whitman, a local billionaire's son and world-class skier. He's beautiful, with his pale face and coal black hair, those bright blue eyes and that deep blue overcoat. He gives me a smile and a wink as I walk past, and I blush slightly while Cindy waves at him.

I wonder what he's doing out watching all this? Is he involved? Is he behind this, maybe? He certainly does seem to be gloating a little. I glance back at him and see that he's wiggling his fingers back at Cindy, his eyes dancing with mischief and good humor. *No way of knowing.*

The Whitmans—just the father and his adult son, as far as I know—live in a giant old house far up the mountainside, and venture down to see us once every week or so. The local rich eccentrics, they are known for their grand gestures around the holidays—such as the massive food donations to the local church that I hope Dr. Whitman will make again. Last time netted each of us enough frozen and canned food to see every poor person in and around Phoenicia through to mid-January.

The elder Whitman is his son's opposite in looks, aside from them both being tall and blue-eyed. Dr. Whitman's complexion is ruddy; his features are generous. He wears a full white beard and mustache, and he always wears a cap over his bald spot, with silver hair flowing from beneath it. Nobody knows why the pair picked a tiny, sleepy town like Phoenicia to settle in, but the kids love them, and they never seem to do any harm.

If the mistletoe prank is their doing, though, this latest grand gesture is ... beyond bizarre.

"I'm cold, Mommy. Can we stop for a cocoa?" The chirpy little voice at my ear drags me back to earth. Cindy's getting big

—I'm strong, but my arm is starting to ache. Still, we only have the one wool blanket to use as a shawl, and I can't wrap it around us both if she walks beside me.

I do a quick bit of poverty math in my mind. A big cup of cocoa with whipped cream and sprinkles for each of us at the candy shop will mean temporary relief from the cold, but no Christmas candy. But I do have baking chocolate, sugar, vanilla, and milk at home.

"Can you hold out until after we get your bunny and go home? If you can wait that long, you can have two mugs of chocolate." Made from scratch, each mug costs maybe forty cents apiece.

I hate having to bargain with my baby daughter over tiny things, but I have no choice. Not even at Christmas. That's just how it is. She'll get two gifts from the toy drive that she won't get to pick, Christmas cookies because I bake them, a five-dollar pizza, one bag of chocolate drops in bright foil for her stocking, and her snow bunny. And then I'll be broke again until my next check, and praying that the Whitmans give us another break.

She lifts her head to peer at me, her dark eyes thoughtful in her round little face. She has her father's looks and his way of drawing her little brows together as she thinks something over. "All right, Mommy," she says very solemnly, and snuggles closer to me. "But hurry up!"

"I'll do my best." The sidewalks are slippery from all the slush from a recent snowfall. The shopkeepers try to sweep the worst of it back into the gutters, but I can feel my worn boot treads slide slightly every few steps. I take deep breaths and fight a surge of panic every time I slip more than half an inch, praying we won't go down in this crowd of shoppers and gawkers.

We're half a block from the toy store when I see a man step out of the tobacco shop two doors down and stop dead for a moment, my eyes widening. It's him—James Norris. Former leading man, billionaire media mogul, and the only man associated with Phoenicia who could give the mysterious Whitmans a run for their money in terms of wealth and success. I've heard before that he sometimes visit town, but I've never seen him myself.

I've had a crush on him since I hit puberty. Now in his forties, he's every bit as hot as he was back when I fell asleep next to open magazines filled with pictures of his tanned and smiling face. His thick brown hair sweeps back from a high forehead; his features are rugged and his mouth generous. His smile is like a flash of light, making his golden-hazel eyes twinkle. Only the slight crow's feet at the corners of his eyes give him away as being over thirty.

He's dressed down today in jeans, snow boots, and a thick Irish sweater in storm-cloud gray. He rocks on his heels as he checks his phone, seemingly oblivious to the gigantic bundle of mistletoe he's just stopped under. We're headed straight for him.

Oh God. For a split second I'm torn between marching up and ambushing him for a kiss that would probably warm me through the next year, and crossing the street just to avoid him. My heart bangs in my ears. I'm suddenly terribly aware of the way my pale blonde hair has slipped loose in wisps from my messy braid, of my cheap lipstick and wind-flushed cheeks.

It's the chance of a lifetime, but weird proliferation of mistletoe or not, I just can't face him.

I take the third option, walking toward him in the crowd, stepping around him politely, and pretending I don't recognize him even though my whole body feels like it's vibrating with rushes of adrenaline. I'm almost past him when I feel Cindy's weight shift. I turn around—just in time to see her lean over and lay a big kiss on James Norris's cheek.

CHAPTER 2

James

I DIDN'T INTEND to go down the hill to town today. It's ridiculous, really, how I ended up wading through Phoenicia's last-minute shopping crowd while everyone else up at Mom's house had all their presents tucked under the tree already. It's my own fault, though. I managed to leave the Tiffany lamp I bought for my mother's collection sitting on my penthouse couch as I left to drive upstate.

MY DISTRACTION WAS UNDERSTANDABLE; my mother *had* just informed me that Andrea, my ex, would be staying with us for Christmas. The smartest thing that surgically-enhanced little gold digger ever did was ingratiate herself with Mom. I've been looking forward to getting away from my New York City problems for a few weeks. It irritates me to discover that one of the worst of them has followed me home for the holidays.

MOTHER HAS NEVER FORGIVEN me for breaking up with Andrea, and has tried to get me and Andrea back together more than once. She doesn't understand that Andrea is a high-maintenance gold digger who whines and nags to get her way and refuses to even contemplate having kids. Even if Andrea wasn't a bitch, she's not the one for me, and both she and my mother refuse to see that.

IN A WAY, the errand is a welcome vacation from the tension up the hill. Andrea, demanding that the heat be turned up to eighty, has spent the whole day since I showed up slinking around in a gold lamé mini dress and matching pumps, with her red hair piled artfully and hard gray eyes ringed with kohl. Clouds of musky perfume follow her around; like her artfully revealing taste in clothes, it once attracted me, but now it makes me a little sick.

I CAN'T BREATHE until I go out. Andrea refuses to go out in the cold with me, for which I'm grateful. The only part of me that still likes her is my cock, and the sway of her hips in that tight, shimmering dress had gotten my libido and me into a hell of a fight on the way out the door. It leaves me distracted and thinking of sex—and wishing I had someone kind and friendly to have a little fun with.

Andrea is a particular type of high-end sex worker who doesn't like viewing herself that way. But her brand of trophy wife isn't there to love your kids, or ease away your stress, or do much of anything besides look good on your arm, spend your money, and fuck. Like an escort. Once I realized what she was truly after—and it took me longer than I like to admit—I tried to free myself of her, but she already had her hooks sunk into my family.

DRIVING HELPS CLEAR MY HEAD. Early winter in New York this year was been short on snow until last week, when we got dumped on for four days straight. Now the worst of it is cleaned up enough for people to move around normally, but the whole landscape on either side of the winding mountain road is blanketed in two feet of white.

I PASS by the Whitman's Dutch revival mansion, an enormous white structure with soaring gambrel roofs, a profusion of columns, and trim in scarlet and green. Even during the day those two have enough lights and decorations that their sprawling front lawn looks like a fairy land. The local kids love it; so do I. Andrea, predictably, called it "garish," but she has all the Christmas spirit of a coal hopper.

Phoenicia has gentrified a little over the years, some of the touristy shops giving way to boutiques and specialty stores. One thing it's always been, though, is big on holidays. But when I pull onto the main street and start looking for parking, it looks just a bit like the Phoenicians have gone overboard. What is with all the mistletoe?

I'M STILL WONDERING about that a half an hour later as I step out of the tobacco shop where I've picked up an inlaid wood desk humidor for Mom's new boyfriend, Mitch. It, and the antique jewelry box I got Mom as a substitute gift, nestle in cocoons of tissue paper inside my shopping bag. I've got nothing to actually do back at Mom's place aside from making small talk and dodging Andrea, so I'm trying to come up with excuses to prolong my shopping trip.

My phone goes off as I step outside, and I sigh and reach into my pocket to check it. My mother's number. Of course. Andrea would never call herself, not when she can get my poor, gullible mom to summon me home for her.

Mom means well. She just desperately wants me settled with a houseful of cute grandkids, and Andrea has lied to her about her intentions this whole time. My mom is a very honest woman who has so little experience with lying that she can't tell when she's being led on. So Andrea uses her, and she argues in Andrea's defense in return.

I tuck the phone back into my pocket, determined to at least have a few more minutes to myself. *I'll tell her I was in the shop buying the humidor.* It's the excuse I gave for coming down here, anyway. I'm certainly not admitting to my mother that I left the lamp she's been coveting for months on my damned couch.

Fortunately, her birthday's in January, so she'll just have to wait to get it then.

Phoenicia is lovely as always. I would settle here myself if it wasn't so far from everything I'm doing. As it is, I've thought seriously about weekending over here in a house of my own. But God, the crowds are thick today. Not that that's any surprise, given the date.

I stand out of the way as best I can, trying to ignore the sharp smell of the mistletoe hanging everywhere. Maybe I can duck into the cafe for some lunch. Or even grab a few more gifts to tuck under the tree. I'm looking up and down the street, weighing my options, when I notice a lovely young mother approaching me.

She's small, youthful, and almost delicate looking, with large, innocent green eyes, wispy blond hair gleaming like spun gold against her pale cheeks, and lips painted a simple pink. I can't see much of her figure under the gray wool blanket she's got wrapped around herself and her child, but that doesn't matter. I'm already charmed. Especially when I notice the lack of a wedding ring.

Behave, I warn myself, though really, the lady's sweet face reminds me of how I've been longing for a little more sweetness in my life. Especially after spending the morning dealing with that bitter, gilded viper that's invaded my mother's home.

The cherub she has with her is dark-haired and olive-skinned, her brown eyes full of wonder at the world as she gazes around. The two of them talk for a moment—and then the mother notices me and hesitates.

. . .

I QUICKLY PRETEND NOT to be watching her, busying myself again with my phone. I text my mother with *"in shop, call soon"* and glance up again, noticing the blonde gazing at me all wide-eyed. I've been recognized.

IT HAPPENS SOMETIMES, even though I've been behind the cameras in various capacities, instead of in front of them, for over ten years. Most people reach a certain level of stardom and wealth and blow it on a lavish lifestyle, drugs, friends, what have you. I invested it, determined to create a production company where I could create good movies without tripping over corporate politics.

Things turned out better than expected. So I've been out of the spotlight for a while, at least on that level. I'm the man behind the curtain now.

BUT NOT TO THIS ONE. I see the old dazzle in her eyes for a moment, and then the most charming attack of shyness that I have ever witnessed. For a moment I wonder if she's going to walk up to me, or run away. I'm disappointed when she lowers her gaze and moves to walk around me instead.

Then the little cherub in her arms, mischief in her eyes, leans over and lays a smooch right on my cheek!

THE POOR WOMAN FREEZES, her eyes flying wide open again, and looks up at me in a panic. I let out a laugh, even more charmed than before, and glance up at the bundle of mistletoe hanging directly over my head. "And a merry Christmas to you too," I inform the little girl, who is grinning hugely.

. . .

"Oh my God," the woman mumbles in such a mortified tone that I want to pat her shoulder and tell her it's okay. I mind her personal space, though, and just maintain my smile and shake my head.

"It's no trouble. She caught me fair and square!" I give the woman a smile, and she starts to relax, seeming a little baffled that this is actually happening. *Poor thing. It's all right, dear, I'm not going to bite!*
Unless you want me to, of course.

There was a time in my career when that starry-eyed look coming from a beautiful young woman would have had me angling to get her into bed. With fans, it's generally fairly easy—and fun for all, at least when I do it. Looking at her and at the soft light in her eyes when she gazes up at me, I'm tempted to do it again.

"Yes, I did catch you," the little one insists, and then says firmly, "And that means you owe me and Mommy a cocoa! The kind with the whipped cream and peppermint sticks!" She even pokes a finger into my chest.

The poor woman. It's all I can do not to laugh as she gives her opportunistic child a look of horror. "I—I'm sorry," she starts, but I just smile and shake my head.

"Don't you worry about any of that. I'm charmed, and fortunately for us all, I could really use the distraction." I gaze down at her as she stares up at me, still slightly starry-eyed. Her little girl is beaming with such deep self-satisfaction that I almost start laughing again. This kid really knows what she's doing.

"My name's James," I say warmly, never breaking the woman's gaze. I've missed having someone look up at me like I hung the moon, especially after Andrea's hot-cold mix of manipulative sweetness and disdain. There's nothing manipulative about this woman. "What's yours?"

"Lorena," she murmurs tentatively, as if she's worried I might be playing a prank on her. "This is Cindy."

"Well, pleased to meet you both," I reply, before gesturing toward the cafe. "Now let's all get a hot drink, shall we?"

CHAPTER 3

Lorena

When we walk in the door of the chrome-countered, checker-floored café, I still don't know whether to reprimand Cindy or thank her. Never in my life would I have dreamed that a man like James Norris would end up taking me out for cocoa, but here he is, holding the door for us.

I set Cindy down with a sigh now that we're out of the cold, and roll my throbbing shoulder before removing the blanket and draping it over one arm. She waits beside me patiently, looking around at everything but staying quiet. I take her hand again and we follow the waitress to a table. James pulls out my chair.

. . .

As I'm sitting down, my mind's eye suddenly conjures Manny sliding into the seat across from me as I scoot in unassisted. He was young and artless, but devoted—the kind of romantic who had trouble expressing it. He forgot to pull out chairs. I wince slightly, and hide my expression by quickly snatching up a drinks menu.

"Clever of them to sell hot drinks in all these different flavors when it's this cold out," James comments as he sits down. He towers over me, even when sitting—a giant compared to me and Cindy. "I understand that Miss Cindy likes the peppermint cocoa. Do you have a preference?"

He's leaning toward me, his voice a deep, friendly purr, and my heartbeat suddenly pounds in my ears. I can't catch my breath. I can smell his musky cologne, and the faint scent of mistletoe still hanging around him. "I ..." I force out, and then look hurriedly down at the menu.

Maybe I should have just kissed him and been done with it. It can't end up more awkward than this.

"I've never had most of these," I admit finally, in a soft, hesitant voice. If we ever go for a treat, I get a cup of something very plain and let Cindy revel in her whipped cream-covered delight. I've never even *heard* of most of these drinks.

"Well, what appeals?" he asks without missing a beat.

· · ·

I look down the list and pick one, a little desperate to avoid trying his patience. "Um ... maybe the salted caramel?"

"Salted caramel it is. Clearly you need a treat too, after carrying such a big girl around all by yourself." His eyes dance even more in person than they used to in my magazines. His charisma pulls at me like a magnet. I might have had a crush on him before, but right now, as I bask in the light of his smile, I forget every one of my problems all at once.

How does he do that?

He orders two salted caramel mochas and peppermint hot cocoa, all in their biggest size, and a plate of fruit turnovers to share. Cindy bounces happily at the prospect, and I have to admit my mouth waters a little too. I can bake pastries, but unless I have a lull between my jobs there's no time to do so.

Immediately after the smiling waitress walks away, his phone rings. "Ah, sorry," he says, fishing his phone from his jeans pocket and checking it. He frowns. "It's family. Please give me a moment."

He turns partially away before putting his phone to his ear. "Yes, hi Mom." A pause. His smile starts to look a little forced. "No, I ran into a friend in the tobacco shop, and we're having a hot drink before I drive back up."

. . .

I TRY to distract myself by looking around, but I'm dead curious, and find myself listening in regardless. There's a certain amount of tension to the long pause that follows as his mother talks, as if he's listening to a lecture. "Mom, look, I understand that she invited herself to Christmas, but that is between Andrea and you. She and I haven't had a relationship in several months."

MY EARS PRICK UP. *What?*

JAMES HAS BEEN LINKED for years to the notoriously high-maintenance model-actress Andrea Case. He has never been seen in public with anyone else. But apparently, all of that came to an end earlier this year, while I was too wrapped up in hustling to pay my bills to keep tabs.

"MOM, please don't let Andrea push you around like that. It's bad enough that she invited herself over for Christmas. This is your home, and I came to visit you. Not her. If she can't handle my leaving for a while, she can always come join me."

The corner of his mouth curls knowingly; Andrea doesn't seem the type to brave the snowy streets of Phoenicia, and it seems that he's counting on that.

So ANDREA IS STILL FOLLOWING him around even though he's told everyone that they are quits. She apparently is conning his mom and is trying to control him. And he's just trying to come down here for a little break or something, but Andrea won't even allow that. I have a nose for putting stories together, and this one has me intrigued.

"Don't let her worry you, Mom, it's fine. I'll be back soon."

He hangs up and puts his phone away, giving me an apologetic look. "Sorry. Family holiday ... things, you know how it is."

"Not really," I reply honestly, which gets me a sharply curious look. "It's just me and my little one here. My husband died two years ago on deployment."

He blinks in surprise, and his gaze sweeps over us again. I brace myself; he's taking in the thin puffer jackets we're wearing, the wool blanket we were using as a shawl, the careful patch in my shoulder bag. I have nothing to be ashamed of; I'm a good person in bad circumstances, and I'm doing the best I can.

But ... what wealthy man ever sees it that way? Aside from Dr. Whitman and his son, of course. But even they're considered eccentric—exceptions that prove the rule. This man, James, whom I've daydreamed about since I was twelve, has no reason to sympathize. No reason not to dismiss me as cheap, lazy, and just a step above a beggar—if that.

My cheeks burn and my eyes sting alarmingly. My stomach shivers with a mix of humiliation and dread. How will he react?

"Ah, well then. That's unfortunate. I thought perhaps that you were here to see relatives." He seems to want to say more for a moment, but then sits back and smiles at the waitress as she brings our drinks. He seems a little relieved by the interruption.

I'm more than relieved. Though after a moment, I realize that the look on his face is more concerned than anything. I push the conversation on to what I hope is more comfortable territory. "So, you're visiting family?"

I KNOW his mother lives in the area. Every local who follows the movie industry at all knows that. But it seems rude to just assume, as if I know about him from anything besides online gossip articles.

"Oh yes," he says, perking up. "My brothers and I visit my mother every year and stay for a few weeks. She's a bit like the Whitmans—she goes mad for Christmas and everything to do with it. Her house looks like a parade float right now."

That makes me smile. "That's adorable." My own house, well ... I just can't afford Christmas lights. We have a tiny tree in the front yard that we trim with peanuts and popcorn and let the birds and squirrels eat, only to string up more the next day. But at night, there's nothing in my yard but darkness.

"I'M sorry if I've brought up something that is uncomfortable for you," he says quietly as he slides our drinks to us. They are each in a huge mug, with a small mountain of whipped cream on top. Cindy's has a candy cane stuck into it, which she eagerly pulls out and starts using like a dipping stick. I make sure I have extra napkins handy for her before turning back to him.

"IT's NOT LIKE THAT. We haven't been on our own very long, and I'm still getting used to Christmases alone." That part's true.

EVEN BACK WHEN my parents were too busy drinking to do

anything, my Aunt Erin would always take over, making sure that I had something to celebrate, at least for a few days. After she passed away, I had one Christmas with Manny before he shipped out. And now it's been two bleak years of Cindy and I fending for ourselves.

I just wish I could give her a better life than this. Cindy is as happy and content as I can manage. Fortunately she's not a demanding kid. But when she gets older, when she's in school, having a poor single mom will weigh against her socially, just as it weighs against me now.

I don't really have many friends in town. Clients, sure. Nobody has a problem with me doing their books, cleaning their houses, or looking after their pets. They will share a church pew with me, a bus seat, or the counter at the cafe. They just have a problem with being seen with me in any situation where we might be taken for ... peers.

Even now, I can see the curious looks from locals and shoppers as they see the three of us together; the plain, slightly ragged girl, her adorable but inadequately dressed kid, and the billionaire superstar. I know what some of them must be thinking: *what's he doing with her?* And it makes me feel a little better, like I'm thumbing my nose at their stupid prejudice.

Relying on charity upstate, regardless of your run of bad luck, wins you no friends, even when you're a war widow. But James isn't from upstate. And as I notice he's still listening to me and has made no move to leave, I really start to relax.

. . .

"Well, that's rather sad. And you live in town, then?" He spoons aside some of his cream to keep it from getting on his nose as he takes a swallow of his drink. "Mm. That's divine. Really, Lorena, you should try this."

I hesitate. It smells decadent enough to make my mouth water, as does the scent of the pastries. I wanted to save it a moment longer, but I need the distraction from the awkward topic.

I scoop up the long spoon and nip up a mix of foam, cream, and caramel drizzle on the end of it. I slide it into my mouth ... suddenly aware of how closely he's watching. I lick the spoon clean, the unbelievable mix of rich sweetness and subtle shifts of flavor melting on my tongue. Then I swallow, taking a little gasp of breath in surprise. "Wow."

His smile widens again. "See?"

"I need help Mommy!" Cindy announces, and I turn at once to help her hold the big mug and avoid getting cream all over her face. She laughs as she gets a little gob on her nose. I hear James chuckling warmly beside us.

I turn back to him and see him looking at us with something I would never have expected. Not pity or amusement, not mockery or barely hidden disdain, but rather ... wistfulness. His eyes are sad, with the warm, longing look of a dog staring after his family's car.

. . .

"What is it?" I ask him gently, suddenly too arrested by his unspoken sadness to care much whether I make a bad impression.

"I'm sorry, I just ... your family may be small, but there's real warmth there. That's rarer than it should be." He tilts his head slightly. "So, what do you do for work?"

I squash a moment of defensive nervousness and answer the question directly. "A bit of everything. I've got a client who I'm a personal attendant for, another one I shop for. I take in packages for a dozen people around town and walk several people's dogs. I house sit in the off-season. Things like that."

I wish I could describe my scramble to get enough work in half a dozen fields as something more glamorous, or at least difficult. But the real problem is cramming in enough hours of such work to make ends meet. Rich people don't stay rich by being generous with the help.

His eyebrows rise. "Oh. Well, you know, if you have a card or something, my mother's been looking for a companion. She's in good health, but she doesn't drive, and she spends too much time up on that mountain eating out of cans."

My heart jumps. I don't care that it's not the kind of relationship I wish I could have with the man. It's the possibility of a solid job with a client whose refreshingly non-classist son seems to like me. "I—of course. Just give me a moment."

I'm fishing for a card in the bottom of my bag, wishing I had slipped more into my wallet, when Cindy drops her spoon. "Need more help, Mommy!"

"Just a minute, hun," I say distractedly as I dig. *Of all the times I've carried these cards around and not needed one, now I need one and can't find it.*

"Here, let me help." James quickly moves to offer his own spoon, and Cindy takes it and happily keeps eating the cream off the top of her cocoa.

"Thank you," I say as I finally find one of my simple business cards and hand it over to him. He accepts it, and I settle back to take a swallow of my own drink.

I try to savor it. It's not just a drink—it's a dessert. This and the turnovers are probably the only real treats I'll get this holiday. Soon, though, if this client comes through, I'll be able to afford treats now and again once more.

"So what kind of help would your mother need?" It's an easy topic to jump into.

"Besides driving into town and occasionally going to doctor's appointments, she spends late winter in Florida and will need a sitter for her house and cats. It's not difficult work; she already has a maid. And she loves kids, so you could probably bring the little princess along." He winks at Cindy, who looks back at him solemnly.

I FIGHT down a laugh at my daughter's deepening frown. "Uh oh. Now you've done it."

CINDY FOLDS HER ARMS. "I'm not a princess. I'm a vampire."

"OH, I'm terribly sorry, my mistake." James puts a hand on his broad chest and I'm all blushes and stifled giggles again, watching. He gives her a confused look. "But if that's so, how can you drink cocoa?"

"COCOA'S YUMMY. Dracula doesn't drink wine cause he wanted cocoa." She carefully lifts the mug in both hands and takes a wobbly swallow, only spilling a little. I swoop in with a napkin before the droplets can run down her chin.

JAMES IS VERY good with her, I think. At least, from what I've seen so far. He also seems very attentive to my moods and needs, which is rare, especially in a stranger.

Is he putting on an act to impress me for some reason? Or is he sincere, and just better at showing it than many?

I REALIZE that not even Manny was this attentive. Manny, who left a hole in my heart the exact shape of his memory, was a soldier, not a gentleman. Quiet, stoic, who prayed more often than he drank, was shy in bed and yet loving, and spent every minute of his life with me that his military commission allowed.

I LOVED HIM. I miss him. But he never had a tenth of the charm of the man across the table from me.

IT'S BEEN two years and change since I've let a man touch me—since I've even wanted a man to touch me. It's only ever been Manny. Movie-star crushes are just a way of letting off steam.

UNTIL THEY'RE in front of you, flesh and blood, friendly and charming as hell, and the possibility of actually going to bed with them becomes a faint blip on the horizon.

WHY ELSE WOULD he be so friendly? Is he just horny, or lonely for someone who won't treat him like this Andrea woman seems to? The idea of his being lonely is a slippery slope by itself. It makes my heart open a crack—and with that comes a surge of guilt, because the man I'm feeling that bit of tenderness toward is not my husband.

TO THIS DAY, I'll never know what secret assignment Manny was on that left him and half his squad dead, with mourning families trapped in the same red-tape nightmare as I. Four of us wives have no bodies to bury, no explanations of what happened. Nothing to show for our loved ones but the government sending empty letters with official words instead of any consideration, financial or otherwise.

How can these men's service not be acknowledged just because the specifics of their mission have to be kept secret? No one has ever had an answer for us. We've been struggling with the help of volunteer attorneys for over eighteen months to get them. But the Veterans Administration has not budged.

The other widows and I still keep in touch. We have an email chain that we share legal information and news on, and chat together. Awkward pen pals scattered across the state, reaching out to each other now and again when the pressure gets to be too much and no one else can understand. It is like having four sisters—sisters in blood.

"I think I could do all of that for her easily. How many hours a day would she need me?" I am praying that his mother will need me a lot. Almost everything else I do can be shuffled around or done on the way to completing other errands. But a solid job where I can bring my daughter? *Where do I sign up?*

"I'll talk to my mother and call you with details," he says brightly as he enters my number into his cellphone. "It won't be more than a day or two."

"Thank you," I murmur, still shocked at the sudden opportunity.

. . .

"Oh, don't thank me. I haven't actually had an uninterrupted chat with someone so pleasant since I got here." He winks. "So perhaps I have a few ulterior motives in recommending you."

"O-oh," I murmur, blinking, my heart pounding again. Cindy takes one look at my blushing face and starts giggling.

If you want to continue reading this story, you can get your copy from your favorite vendor by searching for the title:

The Widow's First Kiss

A Billionaire and A Virgin Romance

Dreams Fulfilled Book One

You can also find the e-book version by typing this link in your computer's browser:

https://www.hotandsteamyromance.com/products/the-widow-s-kiss-a-billionaire-and-a-virgin-romance

OTHER BOOKS BY THIS AUTHOR

Saving Her Rescuer: A Billionaire & A Virgin Romance

I was just trying to get away from my crazy ex for the weekend when I ended up in a giant pileup on the highway up to Gore Mountain.

https://geni.us/SavingHerRescuer

~

Sensual Sounds: A Rockstar Ménage

Lust. Lies. Double lives.

. . .

THE ROCK and roll industry is full of people who are looking out for themselves and willing to do anything to rise to the top.

HTTPS://WWW.HOTANDSTEAMYROMANCE.COM/COLLECTIONS/FRONTPAGE/PRODUCTS/SENSUAL-SOUNDS-A-ROCKSTAR-MENAGE

∽

ON THE RUN: A Secret Baby Romance

MURDER. Lies. Fraud. Just another day in the lives of billionaires and women on the run.

HTTPS://WWW.HOTANDSTEAMYROMANCE.COM/COLLECTIONS/FRONTPAGE/PRODUCTS/ON-THE-RUN-A-SECRET-BABY-ROMANCE

∽

THE DIRTY DOCTOR'S TOUCH: A Billionaire Doctor Romance

I AM A MASTER. An elitist. I am at the top of my field, and I know what I am doing.

HTTPS://WWW.HOTANDSTEAMYROMANCE.COM/COLLECTIONS/FRONTPAGE/PRODUCTS/THE-DIRTY-DOCTOR-S-TOUCH-A-BILLIONAIRE-DOCTOR-ROMANCE

THE HERO SHE NEEDS: A Single Daddy Next Door Romance

HE'S the only man I've ever wanted...

HTTPS://WWW.HOTANDSTEAMYROMANCE.COM/COLLECTIONS/FRONTPAGE/PRODUCTS/THE-HERO-SHE-NEEDS-A-SINGLE-DADDY-NEXT-DOOR-ROMANCE

YOU CAN FIND all of my books here:

HOT AND STEAMY Romance
https://www.hotandsteamyromance.com

Facebook
facebook.com/HotAndSteamyRomance

©Copyright 2020 by Alizeh Valentine - All rights Reserved

In no way is it legal to reproduce, duplicate, or transmit any part of this document in either electronic means or in printed format. Recording of this publication is strictly prohibited and any storage of this document is not allowed unless with written permission from the publisher. All rights are reserved.

Respective authors own all copyrights not held by the publisher.

www.ingramcontent.com/pod-product-compliance
Lightning Source LLC
LaVergne TN
LVHW011726060526
838200LV00051B/3040